ASSASSINS

Assassins

a novel by
Robert Tine

based upon the story by
Larry and Andy Wachowski
and the screenplay by
Larry and Andy Wachowski
and Brian Helgeland

HEADLINE

First published in Great Britain in 1995
by HEADLINE BOOK PUBLISHING

ISBN 0 7472 5356 0

Typeset by Keyboard Services, Luton, Beds
Printed and bound in Great Britain by
Cox & Wyman Ltd, Reading, Berks

HEADLINE BOOK PUBLISHING
A division of Hodder Headline PLC
338 Euston Road, London NW1 3BH

Assassins

Chapter One

———◆———

The two figures looked small and insignificant under the huge gray dome of the autumn sky, both trudging slowly, single file across the vast salt marsh. The man in front was not dressed for a hike in a muddy swamp and he made his way awkwardly, as if unsure of the ground beneath the thin soles of his handmade loafers. The clothes he wore suggested a certain level of affluence and an almost fussy attention to style. The suit was expensive, a well-cut double-breasted silk, slightly flashy, probably Italian. His shirt was ice-white and faultlessly pressed, his colorful silk tie was Hermes, very expensive. The cuffs of his pants were sodden with mud, and with each forward movement he sank deeper into the muck. He muttered under his breath and swiped wildly at the damp air, trying to swat the tiny, almost invisible swamp flies that buzzed up with each step he took.

The man behind him was properly dressed for the hike through the swamp: a pair of well-worn jeans tucked into rubber boots and a denim shirt. He moved easily through the difficult terrain – the flies didn't seem to bother him;

in his right hand he held a pistol, a .22-caliber automatic, the pug nose of the weapon fitted with a silencer as long and as fat as a cheap cigar. The gun rested easily in his palm, as if it were part of him.

The well-dressed man was named Ketcham; the properly dressed man was Rath. Differences of attire aside, the two men had several things in common. Both men were rich. Both men were good at their jobs. Both men were assassins.

A minute or two into the future and one of them would be dead.

There was one major difference between the two men, however – age. Ketcham was older than Rath by a good ten years. His dark hair was shot through with gray and there were two snowy patches of pure white at his temples. His face was deeply lined and the clear signs of a deep fatigue showed in his eyes.

Rath, by contrast, appeared youthful. His hair was jet black, the skin of his face taut, his eyes bright.

Age was at the bottom of the involvement between the two men. Ten years ago – even five years ago – Rath would not have been able to take Ketcham with quite so much ease.

Ketcham took another step and sank ankle deep into the mud. As he tried to pull himself free, the viscous mire seemed to flex like a muscle and pulled his shoe from his foot.

'Aw shit...' Ketcham muttered. He glanced over his shoulder at Rath, who motioned him forward with a slight movement of the gun, as if suggesting that the loss of a shoe didn't matter, as if he wouldn't need them much longer.

Ketcham balanced on one leg, looking down at his

mud-filled shoe, then over at Rath. He smiled. 'When I first saw you,' he said, 'I wasn't scared. I was just wondering why you were dressed like that...' He nodded toward Rath's sensible boots. 'Now I know...'

Ketcham stripped off his dark silk sock and stuck his foot into the mud tentatively, as if testing bathwater. The mud felt good and Ketcham smiled as he thrust his foot deep into it. He yanked off his other shoe and pitched it into the swamp. As he grabbed the other sock, Ketcham lost his balance and sat down in the mud with a splat.

All Ketcham could do was shake his head and laugh. 'This is absurd ... You know, Rath? Really absurd...' Had it only been an hour before? He had been walking from his apartment building to his car, dressed for a night on the town; Rath had come out of nowhere. The instant Ketcham felt the gun in his back he knew it was all over. Checkmate...

Wearily he got to his feet and dug his toes into the dark, wet earth. 'This feels good, Rath. You should try it.'

'Come on,' said Rath quietly.

Ketcham nodded and walked a few feet, enjoying the sensation of the mud between his toes. But after a moment the pleasure began to fade and the awfulness of his situation suddenly seemed to wash over him.

'It's twisted, but I'm honored ... You know?' Rath shook his head again. 'You're the best. They sent the best. It means at least they're still afraid of me.' A slight note of desperation crept into his voice. 'That's gotta mean something, right? They ... I'm still a threat to them.'

Both men knew who 'they' were. Rath did not answer.

Ketcham looked ahead, toward a grove of trees, and started walking toward them. 'Over there, right?'

Rath nodded. 'Right.'

Ketcham was a professional to the last, even to the point of spotting his own place of execution. There was not the slightest possibility that anyone would see them in a heavily wooded thicket in the middle of a remote swamp. Ketcham shuddered at the thought of his body lying in the muck, prey to all the slithering things that dwelled in the ooze. He was going to disappear forever. His body would, in all likelihood, never be found.

'I knew this day would come...' Ketcham sighed heavily. 'But this morning I could have sworn I was going to live forever.' They were only a few steps from the first of the trees. Ketcham's voice grew more desperate. 'Any chance of you telling me who The Contractor was? Huh, Rath?' He wet his lips nervously. 'At least tell me how much I was worth. A dime? Two?' He looked around at Rath. There was fear in his eyes. 'You're not gonna tell me, are you?'

'Does it matter?' Rath asked.

Ketcham thought for a long moment then shrugged his shoulders. 'No,' he said quietly. 'No, I guess not...'

They were well into the trees now. Ketcham did not need to be told, stopping where a dead branch hung from a tree. 'Here?'

Rath gestured with the .22, moving his victim a few steps to the left. The shade of a smile passed across Ketcham's face, a wistful smile, curious and inconsistent with the man. The smile said that he was leaving his last hopes behind.

'We both play the game, Rath,' he said softly. 'Sooner or later the wheel turns.' He stared hard at Rath. 'The wheel turns ... for everybody ... Ever wonder who's got your bullet, Rath? What kind of shoes will you be wearing when the day comes?'

By way of an answer, Rath moved directly behind Ketcham, the perfect position for delivering a single shot to the back of the head. Ketcham winced and began to sweat hard, his fear showing crystal clear.

'Rath, whatever the contract is, I'll double it.' Ketcham's voice was high and tight, shot through with panic. 'Triple it! Just say ... just say you couldn't find me. Take the money and buy yourself some good karma.'

Ketcham was afraid to turn around. He cringed as he sensed Rath raising the weapon and aiming it at the back of his head.

Tears as fat as grapes started rolling down Ketcham's cheeks. 'Oh God! Don't pull yet, not yet!' He was begging for a few moments more, as if something, some miracle lurked just ahead in the future, something that could save him. 'Christ...' He was panting with fear now. 'I've done some bad things in my time. Really bad.'

Random images from his past crowded into Ketcham's brain. He remembered fire and screaming faces, indiscriminate gunfire, the slaughter of soldiers and noncombatants alike in a dozen Vietnamese villages; he saw bodies crumbling to pavement – men who literally did not know what hit them – when Ketcham a half a mile away dropped his mark with a single shot from a high powered sniper's rifle. He could see the faces of men, women ... even children. Those faces were twisted in pain or begging for mercy. He had killed them with hardly a thought. Now his own time had come.

Ketcham could hardly speak now, he was trembling so hard. His words came through chattering teeth, as if he had suddenly been caught in a gust of icy wind. 'I can't die like this. Not like a mark. I'm not a mark!'

And he wept – there was nothing left to say. His tears were hot, passionate tears of self-pity, a man in mourning for himself. For a man like Ketcham – a bad man, a cold-blooded killer for hire – this fit of weeping was the closest he had come to honesty in years, possibly in his entire life.

Rath watched him as he shed his tears for his wasted, misspent life. He was not unaffected by the emotion and he was not without his own peculiar version of mercy. Keeping his .22 steady, the barrel just an inch from Ketcham's scalp, Rath reached into his jacket and pulled out a second gun, a weapon almost identical to the one he held. He chambered a round then expelled the clip from the handle, letting the metal envelope fall to the ground. Then Rath eased the weapon into Ketcham's right hand.

The doomed man blinked away his tears and looked at the gun. It was his own weapon, the very gun he had used to kill dozens of men and women . . . It was also his life, his dignity.

'Hello, old friend,' he whispered, hefting it in his hand. 'One round, right, Rath? Got one round in the chamber?'

'That's right.'

Ketcham didn't even consider trying to use that single bullet to kill his way out of his predicament. Rath had him cold – Ketcham knew that there was no way he could get off a single kill shot before Rath dropped him. No one was that good . . . Not even Ketcham. Rath had given him a way out, a chance for him to die with a scrap of self-respect. He would not, after all, die by the hand of another; he wouldn't die like a mark.

Neither man thought it odd that a gentle sense of serenity passed through Ketcham. He had always known he would die. If he had bothered to think about it, he probably would have realized that this way was exactly the manner of death he should have been expecting.

'Live by the sword, die by it, huh, Rath?'

Rath said nothing.

'Your day will come too, you know. It'll probably look a lot like this one.' It wasn't a threat or a caveat. Merely a statement of fact.

Ketcham sighed. 'Last few years I've been looking for a sunrise,' he said calmly. 'Maybe a sunset is better.'

He raised the weapon to his temple and squinted into the aureate rays of the setting sun, the last thing he would ever see. 'Thanks, Rath,' he whispered. Then he pulled the trigger.

The silencer whispered and the single bullet burrowed into his brain. Ketcham crumpled and slopped into the mud. Like a hunter standing over his fallen prey, Rath lowered his gun slowly, as if Ketcham might suddenly spring back to life.

He drew a deep breath and then exhaled slowly and tried not to look at the dark blood that was pumping into the mud.

Chapter Two

———◆•◆———

Over the years, Robert Rath had traveled millions of miles and had stayed in a thousand hotel rooms. At this stage in his career they had blurred together – each destination looked much like the last; no airline was different from another; each hotel room a carbon copy of the last.

But he had never forgotten a mark. He could see every face, hear every scream, remember the sound of bullet shredding flesh and splitting bone. Sometimes he thought he was living in a shadow world, a place populated only by the ghosts he himself had made. It was all beginning to sicken him . . . After watching Ketcham die, he returned to the latest of his anonymous hotel rooms and wished it was the last one he would see, but he knew it would not be.

As he entered, he glanced at the slim laptop computer that sat on the desk. The prompt was blinking on and off expectantly. The Contractor was summoning him. But Rath ignored the command. Instead, he spread a clean white towel on the coffee table and carefully broke down his .22, examining, oiling and cleaning every piece. His future rested on the precise interaction of these pieces of metal, and he lavished attention on them like an indulgent parent.

There was hardly a weapon on earth that Rath was not acquainted with. From simple, but silent blades, to sophisticated fixed-position heavy weapons, Rath had killed with all of them. In the Army they had even taught him how to form makeshift weapons from common, everyday objects. In Rath's capable hands, just about anything could be pressed into the service of killing: a ball point pen, a credit card, a pair of reading glasses; it didn't take much for Rath to take a life.

But of all the weapons, Rath had a special affinity with personal firearms. He understood guns, handled them faultlessly, knew their quirks and idiosyncrasies the way other men knew their pets.

Still ignoring the baleful blinking on the computer screen, he swept open the curtains and gazed out over the city, leaning his forehead against the cool glass. His room was on the twenty-third floor of a faceless skyscraper, and as he looked down on the miniature cityscape below, he wondered – for no longer than an instant – what it would be like to fall. Would it be liberating? Terrifying? Would anything register, beyond a blast of cold air and a sudden darkness?

He didn't know. He would never know. He had seen death up close far too many times; he knew it too well to have a death wish.

With a sigh, he pulled away from the void and sat down at the desk, staring at the computer with loathing. His fingers danced over the keyboard as he entered a long access code sequence, connecting his computer through his cell phone to The Contractor. A moment or two passed then a line of dialogue scrolled across the screen. It happened so quickly that Rath thought he sensed an anxiousness in The Contractor he had not experienced before. It was like a teenager on a Saturday night answering the phone on the first ring.

Contractor: *Where have you been, Robert?*

Rath typed rapidly: *Sick. The flu.*

Contractor: *I don't believe you.*

If words could be said to smirk, these did. Rath snorted angrily. 'I don't care what you believe. I want out. I've had it.'

Contractor: *I've been sitting on a prime contract.*

This angered Rath further. The Contractor should have known by now that Rath was not the sort of man to beg and pant at the prospect of money.

Rath was well paid for what he did, but the money meant very little to him. He had a fair amount of it, but he never saw it, never spent any of it. The bulk of his fortune was thousands of miles away in an account in an offshore bank, the kind of bank where it never occurred to anyone to ask where the money on deposit came from.

Rath sometimes went days at a time without spending a cent. He paid all his bills with a credit card – no limit on it, of course – but he never saw the statements or accounts. The bills went to The Contractor and were paid without comment. Rath could probably charge a Ferrari on his card and not hear a peep out of his employers.

'Who are you, you son of a bitch?' Rath whispered. He stared at the screen, his eyes burning. Somewhere, out there in the clean and silence of cyberspace, The Contractor was prowling. The numbers and codes that Rath used to gain access to him betrayed nothing, gave not the slightest hint of his whereabouts. The Contractor could be across the street or on the far side of the world.

Contractor: *Interested, Robert?*

At that moment, nothing could have interested Rath less – but he knew that he could reveal nothing of his true state of mind. Knowledge was, after all, power. Like an actor reciting his lines, Rath typed in his response.

Rath: *Send the file. I'll have the estimate tonight.*

Contractor: *I'm worried about you, Robert.*

'You should be,' Rath said aloud.

But he typed: *Don't be.*

Contractor: *Good. You are my number one.*

'I'm flattered,' said Rath as the screen went blank. An instant later the slimline printer yoked to the laptop started to hum as The Contractor began to transmit the file relating to the latest of Rath's marks.

The next to die was a man named Alan Branch. Unlike Ketcham, Branch was not an unknown name. He was famous, rich beyond belief, powerful. The photograph transmitted showed him looking into the camera, his eyes hard and defiant. It was the eyes that Rath studied closely, circling them. As another sheet scrolled out of the machine, though, he lost interest. Alan Branch was as good as dead already, just hours away from being another corpse...

With no real purpose, Rath wandered through the city, the streets enshrouded in a fine mist, yet thronged with people. But there is something about a man alone that inspires mistrust – no one spoke to him and those who did notice him seemed to draw back from him, as if his solitude could prove contagious.

In return, he watched the people who so studiously

avoided him. They streamed by him, laughing or deep in conversation or they walked, anxious to reach their destinations, striding along with a purpose Rath did not have. He was a loner, an outsider. Life in the real world went on but he would never be part of it.

The commonplace and the common places that ordinary workaday people were familiar with were to him strange and foreign spaces. He had wandered into a mall and walked through it as if in a museum, each store an exhibit in the history of the everyday. It was an upscale place, each shop a small monument to consumption and expense. He peered into the window of a clothing store, an expensive boutique specializing, it seemed, in the sale of costly clothes to rich women. As he looked in, Rath could see a customer – she certainly looked wealthy and seemed to have that dose of haughtiness that frequently accompanies affluence – in the middle of berating the young clerk behind the cash register. The older woman did not interest him in the least, but the younger did. He watched as she took the ill treatment with stoicism and resignation. The matron was probably too good a customer to offend and the clerk just had to swallow any pride she might have and take it; she nodded and apologized but the old woman refused to be placated. She turned her back angrily on the saleswoman and, huffing and puffing, returned to the racks of clothing, searching through them aggressively, as if something had been hidden there.

Rath was drawn to the young woman. No one, he thought, deserved that kind of mistreatment for an infraction that must have been trivial. On impulse, Rath pushed the door open and walked into the store – and immediately felt self-conscious and out of place. The older woman glared at him from her redoubt behind the dress rack, annoyed that the store was no longer her own private preserve, the saleswoman no longer her personal servant.

The younger woman did not look pleased either. It had been a long day and a customer coming in so near to closing time was not really welcome. She sighed to herself but managed to smile. The dowager jammed a dress back onto the rack, but the hanger did not catch and the gown fell to the floor. The woman ignored it, but Rath didn't.

'I think you dropped something,' said Rath.

'I beg your pardon?'

'I said, I think you dropped something ... Maybe you better hang it back up.' It wasn't a question or even a suggestion. The woman looked shocked but she did bend to retrieve the dress, roughly hung it on the rack. She cast a cold, withering glance at the clerk and Rath, then hurried out of the store.

'Can I help you, sir?' the saleswoman asked. 'I was just about to close up ...'

The woman was pretty, but she looked tired and there seemed to be a certain sadness in her brown eyes. Suddenly Rath did not want to leave. He did not want to go back out into the anonymity of the crowd.

'I'm looking for something,' Rath stammered. 'I ... I'm not sure what.' Now he was wondering just what the hell he was doing in that place.

The clerk knew the routine – or thought she did. It was part of her job to help floundering males – husbands and boyfriends in search of a present. Every day she guided some hapless man through the mysterious, cabalistic world of women's fashion.

'Some kind of special occasion? Birthday?' she asked. 'Or maybe an anniversary?'

Rath shook his head, not sure of what to say next.

When birthdays and anniversaries were eliminated, there was usually only one other possibility. The clerk smiled knowingly. 'A fight, perhaps?'

Rath started to say something, then stopped; the saleswoman took his silence as an affirmative. 'You said something you regret?'

It took a moment for Rath to find the courage to confess. 'Regret? ... Yes. You could say that.'

'Are you really sorry?'

Rath nodded. He was truly sorry for everything he had done, but she would never know the depths of his remorse.

The young woman plucked a lush, red velvet gown from a rack and held it against her breast. 'Bring this home and she'll say *she's* sorry.' Her smile widened. 'There's a catch...'

'A catch?'

'It's expensive.' She turned the price tag out of the sleeve and showed it to him, assuming the price – it was three thousand dollars – would send him scurrying for the door and allow her to get busy closing up the store. But she was disappointed. Rath didn't flinch at the price.

'She's about your size,' said Rath softly. 'Would you mind...' He gestured awkwardly. 'Could I see it ... on you?'

'On me!' The saleswoman was caught off guard by this request and she was flustered for a moment and she wondered if this would-be customer was actually some kind of weirdo. But she could see in his eyes that he was not – in fact, she felt safe and secretly charmed. Most of all, it would be nice to finish the day with such a lavish sale.

'Give me two minutes,' she said, vanishing into the back room of the store.

It was then that Rath seemed to wake up, wondering if he had suddenly lost his mind. What on earth was he doing in a woman's boutique having a salesclerk model an evening gown for a fictitious love in his life? Yet, as he headed for the door, she stepped out from behind the curtain, and Rath stopped dead in his tracks – the transformation she had brought about in a few short moments was nothing less than stunning. Her shoulders were bare and her smooth skin seemed to have been illuminated by the deep scarlet of the material. She was glowing with beauty.

'Well ... What do you think?'

'It's perfect,' said Rath. His voice was soft and gentle.

'Should I write it up?'

Rath nodded.

She moved quickly, stepping to the sales desk and writing a receipt rapidly, as if she feared he would sneak away if she didn't close the sale quickly.

Rath watched her closely, noticing that there was an open textbook on the desk, a few lines marked with a yellow highlighter. 'College?' he asked.

She nodded and smiled ruefully. 'I can tell what you're thinking ... You think I'm too old. My daughter says I'm too old to go to school ... I just sit in on classes right now. I don't have the money yet for tuition.' The words tumbled out of her in a rush, as if she had to convince at least one person that she wasn't being foolish. 'I have to do something. I don't want to spend the rest of my life selling someone else's dresses. I mean, you're never too old to have dreams, right? It can never be too late to start over, can it?'

Rath looked away, unable to hold her gaze, as if her hopes were dazzling and disheartening at the same time. 'I don't know.'

She could tell that her words had hurt him somehow, and there was a moment of awkward silence. 'Should I wrap it up?'

Rath nodded. 'Yes.'

'I'll just be a moment...' she said, retreating to the back room once again. She stripped off the dress briskly, donned her own clothes and packed the garment, sealing it with a length of silk ribbon and a bow the size of a sunflower. But when she reemerged, the shop was empty. Rath had gone.

'Damn!' she said, throwing the box down on the counter. Then her eyes fell on the textbook still open on the desk. A wad of hundred dollar bills stuck out from the pages.

'Damn...' This time she whispered the word, amazed that a stranger could have done something so rash and generous.

There was a note, a single line scribbled on the back of one of the store's cards. Rath had written: *Your daughter is wrong.*

Rath spent the rest of the night in his hotel room slowly working through the material about Alan Branch that The Contractor had faxed to him. He learned that Branch's personal wealth was estimated to be in the billions of dollars, a vast fortune built through investments in defense, aerospace and cutting edge high-tech electronics. Once he had made his money, he had set about spending it – supporting a dozen unpopular causes around the globe. His name first hit the headlines when, a decade before, he had been called before a Senate subcommittee and accused of having channeled funds into the hands of right wing death squads throughout Central America. The senators had been unable to pin Branch down and no charges were ever brought, but no one who had seen this austere, arrogant man treating the committee, the press and the American people with lordly disdain doubted that Alan Branch was guilty of something. Following his exposure on Capitol Hill, Branch had retreated into an obsessive reclusiveness, hiding himself away in his fabled mansion, insulated from the outside world by layers of flunkies, flacks, lawyers and tight-lipped security operatives. He had not been seen in public for years, and from time to time a rumor went around that he had finally died.

But he hadn't – not yet, anyway.

Now Alan Branch was back in the news. His brother, Samuel Branch, had been killed in a car accident and it was said that Branch was going to emerge from seclusion to attend the funeral. There was no doubt in Rath's mind that the car accident had been no accident, but a carefully planned ruse to flush Branch from his lair. If Branch did appear, then it would be clear that he did not consider himself at risk.

Then Rath would kill him. Why? Why Alan Branch and why now? What part would this action play in some huge global chess game? Rath did not know. Rath killed because he was good at it. It was what Robert Rath did for a living. And because The Contractor had decreed it.

He had worked out his plan – he could see the hit

unfolding in his mind as clear as a movie. It would happen as projected.

He turned on his computer and punched in the long skein of numbers that launched him on the internet and into the den of The Contractor.

When the prompt came up on the screen, Rath logged in and typed: *I have my bid.*

Chapter Three

———◆◆◆———

The Avianca jet touched down on runway thirty-two
more or less on time, close enough to the scheduled
arrival to suit Bain. He was a man of considerable
contrasts. He had an easygoing sense of good humor,
coupled with a vicious temper. He had his own personal
sense of highly idiosyncratic honor, which forbade some
things but did not rule out killing – which was a good
thing, because Bain was a killer, an up-and-coming
murderer for hire.

He made his way through the airport, walking briskly
from the arrival gate to the immigration desk, getting in
the line of non-US passport holders. It didn't take long
before he was face-to-face with the stern-visaged INS
officer. He looked over Bain's stylish clothes and expensive cordovan briefcase, and took in the slight smirk on
Bain's face. The official didn't care for the entire package
and his mistrust deepened when Bain produced a
Colombian passport. He carefully checked the name and
number against the hot list of known felons, fugitives,
political subversives and other undesirables undeserving

of admittance to the United States of America. To his great disappointment Bain's name was nowhere to be found. The immigration officer had no reason to deny him entrance and that pained him. In his book, cocky, rich young men from Colombia could only be trouble – drug trouble.

'Is your visit for business or pleasure?' he asked through clenched teeth.

'Both,' said Bain. And he meant it. He would make a lot of money for killing Alan Branch. And he would enjoy it.

Rath's plan was simple. The best ones always were. He hit a big drugstore downtown and assembled the things he needed for his procedure – a roll of gauze, a box of plaster of Paris, a sling, some bandages – and then returned to the hotel to put together a convincing plaster cast.

Bain was busy too. He patrolled Oakwood Memorial, the cemetery where the Branch funeral would take place. He walked among the gravestones like a jockey exploring the trace before a big race. There was a freshly dug grave, and a phalanx of folding chairs, reserved for family and honored guests, were carefully arranged at the burial site, a canvas pavilion erected behind them in case the weather should turn inclement. Everything was ready for a nice solemn funeral. Bain almost felt bad about messing it up.

'Can I help you, sir?'

Bain turned. An elderly caretaker stood at his elbow, smiling diffidently. Oakwood Memorial was a very expensive cemetery – it drew a better class of corpses –

and the custodian was used to dealing with rich people. They liked to be coddled. But they didn't like to have to pay for it; they weren't great tippers. The old man had long ago resigned himself to the ways of the extremely wealthy. This young man looked rich, but the custodian expected nothing.

Bain returned the smile. 'Help me?' he said. 'Well, I'm looking for someone.'

'If you tell me the name, I'd be glad to look it up for you in the plot book.'

'I doubt if he'd be there.'

'No?'

'You see,' Bain said with a warm smile. 'He's not dead yet...'

'Oh,' said the caretaker. One of the other things he knew about rich people was they could be strange. In other people it was called craziness. In the rich it was known as eccentricity. Whatever the young man meant, it was no concern of his...

The calm of Oakwood Memorial was shattered the next afternoon when the press and the merely inquisitive ringed the cemetery, craning for a glimpse of the mysterious Alan Branch. The police had been delegated to keep the crowds at bay, but there was nothing they could do about the news helicopters that swooped and chattered overhead.

Private security guards – brawny, unsmiling men in tight suits, their eyes obscured by dark, dark glasses – controlled access to the cemetery itself. They were tough guys and would be hard to take in a fight, but not one of them spotted the fake access pass that Rath had mocked up and printed out the night before. He walked through the security cordon, and no one gave him a second glance or thought twice about the plaster cast he wore on his right arm.

Rath had a very low opinion of private security, and their lack of vigilance on this occasion did nothing to raise his estimation. Expensive bodyguards like these were always the same. Huge bruisers, mounds of rippling muscles in tight suits. They looked ferocious, but they had none of the agility that well trained professionals possessed. These men were as limber – in thought and in body – as hippos.

Rath guessed that they were effective at crowd control, but in the case of real, deadly threats – people like Rath – they were useless. They were over-equipped with too much communications gear, they carried weapons too powerful and with too rapid a rate of fire for use in crowds. But worst of all, in Rath's view, was their pride. These guys were self-important, tough guys acting tough for the benefit of their employers and hot-dogging for the public. Rath walked right by them. They ignored him, he ignored them. They were not a threat.

There was a flurry of excitement when Alan Branch himself arrived – an explosion of flash bulbs, a couple of threats shouted from the crowd, but Branch paid no heed to any of it. Only once he was settled in a chair at the grave, a bodyguard on either side of him, could the service begin.

A choir sang 'Ave Maria,' and all through the hymn Rath studied his mark. Branch looked a little older than the photograph The Contractor had provided, but age had not mellowed those eyes. The old man looked straight ahead at his brother's casket, his gaze sharp and cruel and showing not an iota of grief or bereavement. To

Rath, the look in those cruel eyes suggested that Alan Branch thought his brother had shown distinct bad form in dying at all.

When the 'Ave Maria' finished, the priest officiating gestured to the congregation to stand. All except Branch rose – it was then that Rath noticed that Branch was seated in a wheelchair. He wondered how The Contractor had managed to miss that detail. More likely, The Contractor had known all about it but did not consider it relevant. Sitting or standing, Branch would die.

'I am the resurrection and the life, saith the Lord,' the priest intoned. 'He that believeth in me, though he were dead, yet shall he live . . .'

Rath pulled a small piece of tape from the cast, exposing a sliver of the barrel of the .22 pistol. He angled his body slightly, aiming for Branch.

'. . . and whosoever believeth in Me shall never die, but have everlasting life.'

At that moment the sprinkling system embedded in the ground clicked on, showering some of the mourners. All heads turned and there were murmurs of consternation. The priest faltered for a moment, then caught himself, and went on with the ceremony.

'Bad timing,' muttered a man to Rath's left.

Bad timing? Rath, suspicious as always, wondered if it was as simple as that. The crowd had shifted to avoid the streams of water, but Alan Branch appeared not to have noticed the sudden interruption. In fact, it was out of character, but he seemed to have his head bowed in ardent prayer.

It was Rath who noticed the crimson stain spreading across Branch's crisp white shirt, and he whipped around, searching the crowd for the shooter. The throng stood silent, heads bowed, but through the forest of mourners Rath could see a little daylight, a path opened up by the spraying water. And beyond that, behind a chipped gravestone, Rath could see, for a split second, the sun glinting on the barrel of a gun.

Fate granted him no more than a split second to see what was going on, but a series of images were imprinted on his memory. The shooter was young, male, he wore overalls. He was armed with a heavily silenced sniper's rifle, fixed scope.

For a moment, time seemed to stand still. The priest continued to pray, even as Branch sunk further in his wheelchair. The mourners were motionless, their heads bowed.

Then one of the bodyguards noticed his boss slumped in his wheelchair. The man shouted, 'He's been shot! Mr Branch! He's been shot!'

In an instant the crowd panicked, people running and screaming, the squad of bodyguards shoving mourners aside roughly. Rath looked beyond the crowd, his eyes focusing on a man dressed in denim overalls, a young man. He was ambling away from the crazed crowd, as if oblivious to the pandemonium, and he appeared to be a member of the custodial staff, pushing a plastic barrel of newly raked leaves ahead of him. Rath knew in an instant that the man was the shooter who had killed Branch. He was too casual – no one could have *not* noticed the chaos at the gravesite.

Rath angled his body and fired quickly, the shot slamming into the plastic garbage barrel. No one noticed the shot except Bain. He dropped the act immediately, reaching into the tub and pulling out the lethal-looking long-barrelled sniper's rifle, then running and diving as another bullet flew through the air and chipped a tombstone just to his right.

The bodyguards had seen the gun too and were running toward him. Bain steadied his gun and fired three silent rounds. Three bodyguards tumbled, each bleeding from a neat kill shot to the chest. But Bain was confused. Two more bullets slapped into the granite headstone, showering him with stone chips – but he couldn't see who was shooting at him.

A small army of police were advancing on him now and it seemed as if all the handguns in the world were pointed at him.

'Drop it!' ordered one of the cops. 'Drop it now!'

Bain faked a step to the right, and another silent bullet almost took off his ear. He could feel the heat of it on his skin as it whipped by. *Who the fuck was that?* Bain looked beyond the cops – they were no threat – and just couldn't tell who was trying to take him down.

There was only one thing Bain could do, and his strategy was simple. He surrendered. With a grin he dropped the rifle at his feet.

'Looks like you got me, Officer.'

'Shuttup.'

Cops swarmed around him, throwing him to the ground and handcuffing him. Rath watched Bain disappear under a cloud of blue uniforms, the cops blocking his clear shot. 'Move, you sons of bitches,' Rath muttered, sidestepping a few feet, desperate for a chance to nail the shooter. 'Give me a line ... Goddammit, get out of the way...' His finger tightened on the trigger, but he couldn't make himself fire – he couldn't take the risk of killing a cop.

Bain was being hustled toward a police cruiser, a

human shield of cops surrounding him. He had absolutely no fear of the police – he wanted to know who had been shooting at him with such accuracy. Whoever it was, Bain knew he was good. Only the innocent bystanders had prevented the shooter from bringing him down. That fact interested Bain. He was facing an assassin – an expert – but an expert who did not want to risk taking down a harmless onlooker. To Bain's way of thinking, that made the shooter one strange hit man. Assassins were not famous for their sense of compassion.

As he was pushed toward the police car, he scanned the crowd. For an instant he could see a man some fifty yards away, a man silhouetted against the setting sun. Bain squinted into the rays, but he couldn't make out any features. But he knew.

'Rath,' he whispered.

Chapter Four

———◆———

Rath ran for his rental car and fired it up, the car peeling out and hitting the street at speed. As he drove, he ripped apart the two Velcro strips that held the cast together and shook it off. The .22 pistol remained nestled in his hand. He ejected the clip and slapped in a new one, continuing to race down the street. The narrow two-lane avenue was crowded with pedestrians and traffic and the police cars were gone.

Rath swore quietly, then reached under the seat to pull out a handheld police scanner. He turned it on and tuned it through several bands of garbage until he locked on the local police frequency. The murder of Alan Branch had stirred things up considerably and the air was alive with radio chatter. None of it interested Rath until this:

'This is twenty-three. Proceeding to the seventh with suspect in custody. Over.'

The police dispatcher came back almost at once. 'Roger that, twenty-three. Be careful. Lotta interest in that guy.'

'We hear you. Twenty-three out.'

Rath spun the wheel and hung a right, putting his foot

to the floor and weaving through traffic, trying to catch up. He could imagine what the anonymous shooter was planning. He could not allow himself to be taken into custody and questioned. If that happened he would be in deep trouble – not to mention blowing payment on his hitting the mark. If Rath were in the same position, he would try to escape before he got to the police lockup.

Bain, of course, was thinking exactly the same thing. He sat quietly in the back of the police cruiser, his hands cuffed behind him. But he was cool headed – he had been in much tighter corners – and he calmly took stock of the situation. There were two cops in the front seat, separated from him by a thick wire mesh. His .22 revolver and his sniper rifle were up there too and he was itching to get his hands on them.

Up ahead was another police car, siren screaming, clearing a path through the traffic for the killer of Alan Branch. As the two cars blasted down the street, Bain twisted in the seat and looked behind him – the street was clear of other police cars. That was all the information he needed.

He stared straight ahead, apparently having surrendered to his fate. But behind his back he was working to get out of the restraints. It was surprisingly easy. He gripped his left hand with his right thumb and slowly pulled his left thumb out of its socket. The digit folded unnaturally into his palm, narrowing his hand enough to allow him to slip off the handcuffs.

The cop riding shotgun glanced into the backseat and smiled at Bain. 'Not long now, buddy.'

Bain smiled back. 'You said it.' As the cop turned around, facing forward again, Bain swung into action.

Without hesitation he brought up his feet and kicked out the side window, the glass shattering into a thousand tiny pieces. Before either cop could react, Bain thrust his hand through the broken glass and reached through the driver's side window, grabbing the cop behind the wheel around the neck.

'Jesus Christ!' one of the police shouted. 'What the fuck is—'

Bain had a death grip on the driver, closing his windpipe and putting pressure on his spine. As the supply of oxygen to his brain dwindled down to nothing, he lost control of the car. The cruiser careened crazily, slammed into a row of parked cars, straightened for a moment before cartwheeling end over end and landing on its roof. It skidded across the asphalt, throwing up a torrent of sparks.

All was silence for a moment, a silence made more profound by the terrible screech of tortured metal that had preceded it. Then one of the dented doors opened and Bain emerged, unharmed except for an unpleasant cut on his forehead, just beneath the hairline. He reached back into the cruiser for his rifle and pistol, pushing aside the bodies of the cops, both of whom hung upside down, still strapped into their seats. The driver was dead, his head loose on his neck – Bain honestly didn't know if he had broken the man's spine or if it had happened in the crash – but the other one was still alive.

'Help me,' he muttered. There was blood all over his face and a large chuck in the dashboard where his head had hit.

'I'm busy,' said Bain. He knew he wasn't out of the woods yet.

The cops in the lead police car had realized that the rear

car had cracked up. They hit the brakes, threw the car into a tight, tire-burning turn, and screamed back toward the wreck. The driver was doing his best to control the car and speak on the radio at the same time.

'Officer down! We need an aid car now! Twenty-seven hundred block. Victoria Avenue. Move it!'

Rath heard the call and pushed his foot to the floor. He had to get there before the cops did.

The lead car was racing back to the scene. 'Request backup and ambulance to...' Suddenly the windshield shattered and a slug slammed into the driver's chest. A second later another shot hit, taking out the driver's partner.

Bain was pleased. It was pretty good shooting and he was proud of himself. The last living cop saw his brother officers die in the other car and looked at Bain. 'Don't shoot me, please,' he begged. 'Please ... I got kids...'

'Okay,' said Bain amiably. He rolled clear of the upside-down wreck and watched as the cruiser slammed into the car. There was a horrific crash as the two cruisers hit, metal tearing, glass shattering. The cop was killed instantly and Bain was long gone.

Rath was on the spot a few seconds later. The scene was both eerie and bloody. Two demolished police cruisers and four dead cops – the only sign that Bain had been there at all was a discarded pair of denim overalls tossed on to the sidewalk. The air was filled with the sounds of screaming sirens – Rath would have to move fast. He gunned the engine and turned left, sweeping down the avenue and coming to a halt behind a yellow cab stopped at a red light. Rath had an idea.

He stepped on the gas pedal and the car leaped

forward, giving the cab a good, hard jounce as the two bumpers collided.

The driver was out of the cab in a heartbeat, striding toward Rath, fists clenched. 'There better not even be a scratch, you dumb son of a—'

Before he could say another word, Rath punched him out, knocking him cold with a single, powerful short thump. The cabdriver never saw the blow that laid him out, and Rath caught him before he hit the pavement, then dragged him to the safety of the sidewalk. He relieved the driver of his cap and stuffed two $100 bills into the pocket of the man's T-shirt.

'Sorry about that,' said Rath. 'But I need your cab.' He slipped behind the wheel and zoomed away. He drove aimlessly, taking care to stay clear of the police cars that were racing around the city like a swarm of agitated bees. He could imagine the confusion and commotion that the events of the day had touched off – a dead tycoon and four cops murdered – that was a hell of a big bite to swallow all at once, and there were probably all kinds of pressures on the cops to wrap this one up quickly. But running around helter-skelter like that was the one sure way to achieve nothing.

As Rath drove, he turned his mind to a more interesting question. Who was he chasing? Who was the assassin? He assembled all that he knew about the man: he was young, he looked Latino, possibly Italian – Alan Branch's unsavory connection to South America suggested that the former was more likely. And the kid had guts. It took a lot of nerve to stroll into a situation like the funeral, ice Alan Branch and then get himself out of police custody in a matter of minutes. And there weren't a lot of people in the world who would kill four cops without a second thought or with such apparent ease. The man was a stone-cold killer.

How had he known that there was a bid on Branch in the first place? In all of his dealings with The Contractor, Rath had never done anything to compromise security. The contract must have come from the source, from whoever ordered the hit in the first place. A little insurance, perhaps, or maybe this kid was cheaper than Rath.

The radio mounted on the dashboard of the cab crackled into life, the dispatcher's voice gruff and blunt. 'Who's near Adams and Nine? I gotta fare going to the airport.'

Rath picked up the microphone, glancing at the driver's identity number on the dash. 'This is five-o-one,' said Rath quietly. 'I got it.'

'Okay. Out.'

Now it was time for some answers to the questions. He really wanted to know who was shadowing him. Yet, whatever the reason, Rath had only one goal in mind. He had to find this kid and kill him before he caused any more trouble.

Chapter Five

◆━◆━◆

The Alibi was a run down gin mill, a mean, rough bar, a hangout for small-time crooks, nickel-bag drug dealers and cheap hookers. Once or twice a year it was the scene of a murder, and the killings always touched off calls from neighbors that the joint be closed, but somehow it survived like a weed. The Alibi stood at the corner of Adams and Ninth Streets.

Rath drew the cab up to the curb and waited, engine idling. A few moments later the door of the bar swung open and a couple – a fat man and a blowzy blonde – staggered out, making their way erratically toward the cab.

'Damn,' Rath whispered aloud. He couldn't believe that he had missed his mark. But just at that moment the left-hand rear door opened and Bain slid into the backseat. He was carrying his rifle wrapped awkwardly in his jacket and he had a look of fatigue in his eyes, and the cut on his forehead throbbed painfully. As the door slammed shut, Rath checked the rearview mirror. A cloudy bulletproof partition separated the two men but he knew in an instant that this was the man.

Bain could tell that the driver was checking him out in the mirror. 'There a problem here, mister?' he snapped.

Rath stayed cool. 'The airport, right?'

'Right,' said Bain.

'No problem.' Rath yanked the car into gear and took off. They drove a couple of blocks in silence, Rath glancing from road to mirror. All the while, Bain stared out the side window, thinking about the day just passed. It had been a hell of a ride, but he was going to walk away free as a bird. He couldn't suppress a chuckle, even though it made the cut on his head hurt even more.

'You're cut,' said Rath.

Bain touched the wound and glanced at the sticky blood on his fingertips. He seemed a little surprised that the gash still bled. 'Yeah ... nothing to worry about,' said Bain, smiling. 'I had a little accident at work.'

'What kind of work would that be?'

Bain's mask of amiability dropped away quickly. 'Look, I'm – how do you say? – dead tired. Save the chitchat for someone else, okay?'

Rath nodded. 'Sorry.'

The cab rolled through an intersection and right by the airport exit. Bain sat up, startled, and leaned on the bulletproof barrier.

'What the hell are you doing?' he demanded.

'What?' said Rath, doing his best to act innocent.

'That was the turnoff for the airport.' He half turned in the seat and pointed behind. 'Back there.'

Rath didn't appear to be interested and he made no

attempt to slow down or turn back. 'Sorry,' he said. It didn't sound like a very convincing apology. In fact, Rath was doing his best to act like he couldn't care less – he wanted Bain good and rattled. Angry people tended to make mistakes.

'Sorry? Yeah, well you just blew your tip, pal. You can be sure about that.' Bain rapped his knuckles on the partition. 'Now, get me to the airport.'

'What?' said Rath. 'You think I'm running you up?'

'Just do your job, man,' said Bain angrily. 'Enough of this shit.'

Rath's answer to that was abrupt. He stood on the brake and the cab lurched to a halt next to the curb. They had stopped adjacent to a small park. The playing field was floodlit with a spirited coed soccer game in progress.

'What the hell are you doing?' Bain demanded again.

Rath slapped the car into park and turned in his seat, his right hand gripping his pistol tight. 'Get out.'

'What?'

'I said get out.'

'What the fuck?'

'You think I'm running you up? Get outta here.'

'You can't do this. You can't just—'

Rath cut him off. 'The hell I can't! Get out!'

First Bain was stunned, then angry ... then he started to laugh. 'I don't believe this.'

'Believe it. Now, get out.'

Bain started to open the door of the cab. Once he was outside, it would be an easy matter to blow the guy away and steal the cab. Six hits in one day ... that would be his personal best. Rath was waiting for him to get out of the cab too. He was going to drop him with a single shot and end this messy little episode.

With one leg out the door already, something made Bain stop. He turned and peered through the muddy bulletproof plastic, looking for the driver's ID card. It wasn't in the plastic holder on the dash and Bain thought that was pretty peculiar.

'Where's your license?'

'What you gonna do? Turn me in?'

'I might.' Bain was studying Rath's eyes in the rearview mirror. They were hard and steady. Not the eyes of a cabdriver, he decided. They were the eyes of an ... assassin.

Bain cackled with delight. '*Cojones de Dios!* Robert Rath!'

The cab rocked as both men went for their guns. The rifle was awkward in the cramped space, but Bain used the open door for a little more room to maneuver. They were drawn on each other, a classic standoff. For a second it looked as if Bain were going to make a run for it, but he checked himself.

'I get out, I run – pow, you got me.'

'Take a chance,' said Rath. 'Find out.'

'Uh-uh,' said Bain. He pulled the door closed and lounged on the backseat. 'So now what, Rath?'

'Who are you?'

'*Cono!*' Bain shook his head and grinned. 'The great Robert Rath wants to know me! I can't believe it! This is a big moment in my life, man. I hope you realize that.'

Bain had been hearing about Robert Rath for his entire professional life. Among assassins, Rath had become a mythic figure, an olympian who had become so legendary some were beginning to doubt if he ever existed. No one could be as good as Rath's reputation made him out – but now Bain realized that he was exactly that good. It did not occur to Bain to be frightened about going up against the best. He was brimming with self-confidence.

'Who are you?' Rath asked again.

'Bain,' he said with a grin. 'Miguel Bain...' He laughed aloud. 'I don't believe this. You rolled some cabby, then waited for the right call. That's genius, man. *Genius* ... And then you got the balls to sit there and bullshit with me.' He shook his head slowly, a look of disbelief on his face. 'There's no way I could have done that, man, no way.'

Bain's name meant nothing to Rath and he stared at him hard, holding the gun on him, his hand as steady as a chunk of granite. 'You stole my contract,' he said slowly. 'How did you find out about it?'

Bain didn't answer immediately; he was examining Rath's gun. Hero worship was beginning to show through – in some twisted way Robert Rath was Bain's model of what every good assassin should be.

'A silenced Smith & Wesson .22. Classic,' he said, his voice filled with admiration. 'I switched when I heard that's what you use.' He tapped the rifle. 'Excuse this. I had to use it. It was a long shot, you know.'

Enough of this bullshit, Rath thought. 'Who contracted you to hit Branch? I want some names. Now.'

By way of reply. Bain rolled down the window and looked thoughtfully at the kids playing soccer on the field in the park.

'Listen, Rath ... Why don't you drive around? We can get acquainted. A little chitchat, you know?'

'We'll sit,' said Rath. 'Understand?'

Bain shook his head slowly. But he was pretty sure he knew how to gain the upper hand on Rath. He pointed the barrel of the gun out of the window, resting it on the edge of the door. Before Rath could do anything, Bain fired. The soccer ball exploded in mid-air, tattered bits of leather showering down on the confused kids.

As might be expected, the soccer game came to a sudden and abrupt halt. The players stood still for a moment, then they all started running, converging on the spot where the carcass of the ball had come to rest. The first children to arrive, picked up the ball and examined it closely, passing it from hand to hand. They had puzzled looks on their faces and appeared perplexed, as if the ball was something strange and mysterious that had fallen from the night sky.

'Drive, Rath,' said Bain. He cocked his chin toward the players on the field. 'That kid, number thirteen – she looks tired. Maybe she needs a rest. I could arrange that.' His finger curled around the trigger and he moved the gun slightly, drawing a bead on a girl, following her as she raced down the soccer field.

'Help me out, Rath,' said Bain. He squinted down the barrel. 'A moving target. That's the front sight, right? Or do you just want to drive?'

Rath bit his lip, threw the car into drive and took off, moving fast enough to keep up with traffic but not driving in any manner that might attract attention. Bain chuckled. 'You see, Rath, I know how you think ... Protect the innocent! That's so weak. You could've had me in the cemetery. I was dead meat; all you had to do was ice a couple of cops to get to me. But you couldn't do it, could you? Couldn't shoot the cops. You're *antiquado*, Rath.'

'You've got a lot to learn,' Rath grumbled.

Without warning, Bain raised the rifle and fired, the mouth of the barrel just inches from the bulletproof partition. The rear of the car filled with acrid smoke, but the barrier held – the bullet did not penetrate.

Bain coughed through the smoke. 'Sorry about that, Rath. I had to try.' He shrugged. 'I mean, who knew this stuff really *is* bulletproof?'

Two police cars screamed by, going top speed in the opposite direction, sirens wailing and lights flashing.

'Woah,' said Bain. 'They looked pretty pissed, huh?'

'I wouldn't be surprised.'

'How'd you like the cemetery?' said Bain. 'Pretty good, huh?' Bain relaxed, stretching out on the backseat. 'Course, I had a precedent ... Rome, 14 BC. They killed a general, Flavius his name was. He was at his brother's funeral. Trouble was, I couldn't wait for Branch's brother to die. So I killed him too.' He giggled and grinned. 'Proud of me?'

The whole thing sickened Rath, but from a professional point of view he was impressed with the skill of his rival. But that was beside the point. Right now the only thing that interested him was figuring a way of taking Bain out – quick, quiet and once and for all.

No such lethal thoughts were going through Bain's mind. He almost seemed to be sincere in his belief that the two men could actually become friends, at least until such time as Bain was forced to kill Rath. He had not been kidding when he said he wanted to drive around and chitchat, regaling Rath with old war stories.

It was plain that Bain had a certain crazy feel for history, adapting and reworking it as he needed. 'I killed a guy in his bathtub once. It was a bitch, but I wanted to do him like Marat ... You know, the French Revolution.'

Rath did not react. He knew the famous painting by David of Marat in his bath, dead at the hands of Charlotte

Corday, but he was damned if he was going to give Miguel Bain the slightest satisfaction.

The idea of recreating a death in tableau like that was strangely repellent to him. Killing was a skill, a science – but it wasn't an art.

The young man looked a little disappointed. He stretched and sighed. 'Well . . .' He had the attitude of a man who knew he had to get back to work after a quick coffee break. 'It was nice meeting you, Rath. Someday I'll tell my little *nietos* about this.' It was time. Their friendship had been brief but satisfying. Now he had to kill Rath.

Moving like lightning, Bain slid across the seat, pushed the rifle out of the window and angled it toward the front passenger side window. The first shot blasted out the glass, but the impact deflected the slug. As Bain moved the rifle in for a better shot, Rath yanked the steering wheel, sending the car slinging across the yellow lines into the path of oncoming traffic, the cab veering wildly almost out of control. Bain hung on, though, firing wildly, shots drilling the roof above Rath's head, filling the compartment with caustic smoke. Another shot smacked into the windshield and shattered it, the sudden influx of rushing wind blowing away the smoke.

The lights of an oncoming car stabbed through the smashed windshield, the horn screaming. Rath wrenched the wheel hard to the right, throwing the car back on to the correct side of the road, slamming into a city bus, the force of impact ripping the rifle from Bain's hands. The faces of terrified passengers appeared in the bus windows. The driver fought to control the lumbering vehicle, desperately trying to get the machine back on course.

'*Hijo de puta!*' Bain screamed as his beloved weapon hit

the street and was crushed under the heavy wheels of the bus. He was lucky the bus didn't tear his arm off, but he didn't care. His gun was gone – he was now, officially, a sitting duck.

Rath gunned the engine, raced a few yards then pumped down hard on the brakes. Bain was thrown forward, first smashing into the bulletproof divider, then landing in a heap on the floor of the cab. Rath was out of the cab in a second, the .22 in his hand, cocked and ready. Bain had about three seconds to live – and he knew it.

'Rath, man, don't be like this—'

Just as Rath raised the gun, the air was split with the whine of police sirens, and two cruisers raced down the street toward them. Rath couldn't execute Bain in front of a bunch of cops and expect to get away. There was only one thing he could do.

Gritting his teeth, he got back in behind the wheel and hit the gas hard, racing away. Bain was delighted and he chortled happily as the car roared through the night, the police cars in hot pursuit. 'I love the police!' he yelled. He clapped his hands loudly. 'Hey, Rath! Guess what? We're on the same side! We're teammates! We're *compañeros!*'

Chapter Six

⸺⸺◆⸺⸺

The two police in hot pursuit were just the leading edge of the force that was chasing Rath and Bain. Squad cars had been alerted all over the city and a helicopter was already in the air, streaking through the night sky.

Rath pushed the old taxicab up to its limit, the police cruiser staying right on his tail. Bain looked over his shoulder and frowned at the pursuer.

'Come on, Rath,' he said. 'You get rid of him.'

Rath shoved the car into a hard left-hand turn, a tire-burning, brake-blazing maneuver, the taxicab barreling across the asphalt. The rear of the machine shimmied and fishtailed for a second, then the tires gripped and the car vaulted forward. The move had been so sudden and so unexpected that the two police cars were taken completely by surprise. They raced by, missing the turn entirely, giving Rath and Bain precious minutes of escape time.

As the car roared away under a viaduct, Miguel Bain nodded to himself, appreciating the finesse Rath displayed in losing their pursuers – even if it was only a temporary setback for the police.

'Pretty smooth, man. Pretty smooth for an old man.' He laughed aloud. Rath displayed no emotion.

But Bain knew that they wouldn't have this kind of luck all night, and there was a lot of information that he was curious about. It wasn't often you got a chance to have a sit-down conversation with a living legend like Robert Rath – even if it was at high speed. Bain turned chatty.

'You know, before I went freelance, I was an exchange student.' He laughed at his own joke. 'Yeah, that's right ... CIA University. That's where I first heard about you. Robert Rath – you were a legend around Langley. Those spooks there, they respected you – even if you were Army.'

Rath had known for a long time that to the CIA the uniformed services were beneath contempt.

A police car blasted out of a side street and screeched to a halt across the road, a makeshift roadblock standing between Rath and freedom. Rath's foot never touched the brake. For a split second it looked as if he were going to ram the police car – even Bain looked worried – but at the last possible moment he yanked the wheel and jammed the car up onto the sidewalk and blasted around the squad car.

Bain let out a delighted wail and pounded his fists on the bulletproof partition. 'Can you feel it, Rath?' he screamed. 'It's real! We're alive.'

'Don't count on it.' A high-speed car chase with half a city police force on his tail was not Robert Rath's idea of a good time.

'Awww, you worry too much ...' Bain turned conversational again. 'At Langley, I studied everything you ever did – at least, everything the CIA would tell me about. *Goddamn you were good!'*

Rath glanced in the rearview mirror. There were two new cop cars behind him, moving up fast. Bain studied the road ahead. 'I know this neighborhood. Turn in here.'

There was no reason to question this advice. So Rath pushed the taxicab into a sharp right. They were under the viaduct again, a concrete-and-steel tributary of a larger highway system that encircled the city.

'Yeah ... they said you were the best. Your only competition was that Russian. What was his name? Talinkov ... Nicolai Talinkov.'

The name hit Rath like a hammer. He took his eyes off the road long enough to shoot a questioning glance at Bain.

'Tachlinkov,' Rath corrected. 'How did you hear about Nicolai?'

Bain shrugged. 'A story like that ... it's bound to get around in the business. Doesn't matter how top secret it is, it's too good a story, you know?'

'Tell me the story.'

'They said he shaded you. Over and over,' said Bain, as if telling an assassin's fairy tale. 'And in the end, he aced you. Shaded and faded ... They say he's living on some Greek island somewhere, but I say you were the best. I say Nicolai is as dead as a *clavo* ... That's a doornail. Am I right?'

Rath did not answer and he tried to keep his focus on the situation at hand – eluding the police – rather than messing up his mind with the complicated and un-resolved dilemmas of the past.

'I heard you guys played chess,' said Bain. 'That you

used to send each other your moves coded in the obituaries in the *New York Times...*'

Suddenly, Rath felt as if his past were chasing him as hard as the cops in the patrol cars behind him.

'Don't bother to deny it, Rath ... 'Cause I found it. I had to go through ten miles of microfilm, but I found it. The last game ends before anyone wins.' Bain laughed and shook his head. 'Nicolai thought you were his friend, didn't he? That's how you got him, right? You got close to him and when his guard was down – bam! – ice.'

For a moment it looked as if Rath were going to reply, to set Bain straight on what exactly did happen all those years ago. But before he could say a word, an enormous garbage truck pulled out, blocking their path. Rath jammed on the brakes, whipping the wheel a hard right, power gliding into a grinding U-turn.

The speed of the cab had decreased enough for Bain to make his exit. 'Rath, it's been fun, but I gotta go...' He yanked on the door handle and pushed the door open, but before he bailed out he smiled and winked. 'Hey, Rath, black queen to king's bishop four!'

That said, Bain threw himself out the door, hitting the roadway and tumbling head over heels. Rath watched him in the rearview mirror, thinking about what the young man had said. It all meant something, but it hadn't unfolded quite the way Langley legend had it. There was no time to go over the old ground now.

Without warning, the taxicab was bleached white by a powerful beam of light from above. Over the roar of the engine of the cab, Rath could hear the clattering of the helicopter coming in low and tight, boxing him in the glare. The first thing he had to do was lose the chopper – only then could he disappear.

Abruptly, Rath rammed down on the brake, jinked the car to the left and vanished down a side street. The helicopter pilot was taken by surprise by the move and overshot the mark. Rath could see the huge pool of blinding light racing on ahead out into the darkened suburbs.

Another turn, softer this time, and the cab slid to a ragged stop in a parking lot. Rath grabbed his weapon, opened the door and calmly faded into the night...

Chapter Seven

———◆———

B^{*lack queen to king's bishop four.*}

B Rath turned on his laptop computer and slid a disc
into the A drive, waited a moment while the machine
displayed the document. The first line read: *Game started
May 5, 1980.*

A black-and-white chess board unfolded on the screen,
pieces moving into place, following paths laid down
fifteen years before. A series of dates scrolled across the
monitor – it had taken six months to evolve to this point,
a subtle cat-and-mouse game played out in code, a
schematic representation of the deadly competition that
each man played out in real life. Rath studied the screen,
reliving each move on both sides. It was apparent that
the game was approaching a critical juncture, both foes
circling for the kill.

'Fifteen years and I still remember,' Rath whispered,
his eyes fixed on the screen. 'Those were good moves,
Nicolai. You were the best.'

The prompt on the monitor pulsed, as though to taunt
him: *Enter next move . . .*

Rath was stumped. He recalled this point in the game; it had been Nicolai's move and he couldn't fathom what the Russian was going to do next.

Chess required more than mere skill. You needed to be able to think like your opponent, anticipating his moods as well as his moves. You had to know his loves, his hates, even his sense of humor. You had to be able to see into his mind as if looking into a pool of clear, still water to spy what lurked at the very bottom.

Rath and Nicolai had been friends – if men in their peculiar profession could be said to be friends – but Rath had never been able to fathom him. He could never anticipate his next move in life, rarely in the game of chess.

He inhaled deeply and entered the move Bain had given him. 'Bishop takes rook pawn,' he said quietly.

The response from the computer was instantaneous. The bishop moved diagonally across the screen and erased the pawn. There was a beep from the speaker and the machine declared the result of the move. *Game in check* ...

Rath was taken completely by surprise, not quite able to believe what he was seeing. The move and the result were so unexpected he could feel a mild wave of shock shimmer through him. It was not the surprise of losing a chess game, it was what it meant.

Bain had found the game and Bain had devised the last move. It was a challenge, a gauntlet thrown down. It was a warning. Bain was saying, quite clearly: I am going to kill Robert Rath.

'I'm a mark,' Rath said under his breath. 'A mark...' Suddenly he had an inkling of what Ketcham must have felt like when he first saw Rath, gun in hand.

His eyes never left the screen. 'And who the hell is Miguel Bain?'

Rath wiped the chess match off the terminal screen, fired up his modem and punched in the lengthy series of numbers and codes that would connect him with The Contractor. He was on-line in an instant, again, almost as if he had been anticipating his call.

The Contractor: *Hello, Robert.*

Rath typed quickly, pounding the keyboard a little harder than he needed, as if to put more force behind his words. *Who the hell is Miguel Bain?*

The Contractor: *That's no way to talk to a lady.*

Rath was in no mood for jokes. *Who?*

The Contractor's answer was bland and offhand: *The name of Bain is not familiar.*

'Are you setting me up?' Rath said aloud. 'Is that how it went, Nicolai?' He typed hastily. *Bain was there. He stole my contract. He hit Branch. I want to know who he is.*

The Contractor: *I'll make inquiries, Robert.*

Rath's laugh was hollow. 'I bet you will.'

A number two, followed by a lot of zeroes zipped across the screen. *$2,000,000. That's the bonus on the next contract.*

'Like hell,' said Rath. 'I quit. I'm gone.' His fingers were on the keyboard, ready to disconnect from the web, but he hesitated. He was not a greedy man, but he was going to need something to live on. His skills, while highly developed, were hardly marketable.

The Contractor: *Robert? Are you there?*

Two million was a good score, enough to see him through, enough to insulate himself from his old life. 'Two million...' Rath muttered. 'Two million and I'm gone.'

Rath typed: *Location?*

The answer came swiftly. The Contractor was all business now. *Seattle.*

Rath: *The mark?*

The Contractor: *Surveillance expert.*

Rath: *Action?*

The Contractor: *Selling a synthetic heroin formula to a Dutch buyer.*

Rath paused a moment, digesting this information. Synthetic heroin . . . why would anyone bother with synthetic heroin? The real stuff was plentiful and cheap. Rath figured that someone must have heard that the poppy crop in Burma, Cambodia and Thailand – the so-called Golden Triangle – was poor this year.

He typed again. *Conditions?*

The Contractor: *Retire the mark, retire the buyer and retrieve the information. A computer disc.* A series of documents began to flood the screen, complete files on a group of men, along with photographs of an angular-faced Dutchman and his cohorts. The files were all-encompassing – except for a single detail.

Rath: *Where's the surveillance jacket on the seller?*

The Contractor: *A ghost. All we have is an internet logo.*

The transmit prompted again; the screen turned black except for two eyes, the emerald-green slits of the irises of a cat. Under that was the legend MEOW®comsat.net.

Those eyes belonged to Pearl, a blue point Siamese cat, and they were presently engaged in watching, with great interest, a remote-control toy dump truck. It hummed quietly across the tiled kitchen floor carrying a cargo – a bowl of tuna fish. Pearl could smell the fish and any scurrying thing like the remote-control truck would be likely to intrigue her. The cat chased the truck across the floor, then stopped and appeared to lose interest and turned to grooming herself, meticulously licking her tongue over the silver-brown fur of her breast. Chasing after food was beneath her dignity and it had only been a temporary lapse of judgment that had set her off like that.

Pearl looked up from her task as the truck backed up, the fish tantalizing under her nose. Suddenly she pounced, her sharp teeth sinking into the soft fish. She ate quickly, pausing only to look up after every mouthful to see what her mistress was up to.

Her owner, an attractive, slender young woman, put down the remote and knelt down to her cat, stroking the smooth fur and feeling the ripple of the animal's muscles under her hand.

'Mmmmmmm, hungry Pearl,' she said. 'Eat up.'

She rose and went to the kitchen counter to check on the progress of the coffee that was dripping through the filter of the coffeemaker. 'Almost,' she said, looking down at the cat. As she waited, she opened an envelope of photographs from the local One Hour Photo establishment and carefully examined all thirty-six exposures. Every single one of them was a picture of Pearl. Pearl sleeping. Pearl playing. Pearl just sitting around – to an outsider they were all more or less alike, but to the young woman each was a unique study in the character of her cat.

She selected one and displayed it. It was a three-quarter view of Pearl curled up in a comfortable-looking, overstuffed armchair. 'I like this one, baby. You can see your good side.'

The coffeemaker beeped discreetly – the coffee was ready. She poured herself a cup and sipped, sighing with satisfaction. She leaned forward and looked out the window. Morning was Electra's best time of day – it became her – and the soft light seemed to make her skin glow. The sunlight hit her mane of coppery hair, giving it a gentle radiance as it fell to her slim shoulders in soft waves.

Electra sipped her coffee and looked out of the kitchen window. Her apartment building was identical to the one next door, a completely average, hardly-worth-a-second-glance, six-story apartment block. The whole neighborhood was like that: middle income, middle class, middle of the road. There had been a time when it looked as if the community was going to undergo gentrification, taking a step up the real estate ladder. But a single development stopped the tide of new money dead. On the hillside just a few yards from Electra's kitchen window stood three huge transmit towers, gray steel behemoths that rose hundreds of feet in the air, and each tower was capped by the enormous black bulk of a microwave transponder dish. People didn't like to live around things like that – but Electra didn't mind. In a funny kind of way, the towers reminded her of who she was and what she did. They even hinted at her own, very odd 'hobby.'

Electra liked the neighborhood just the way it was. Quiet, anonymous, peaceful – where all the residents more or less kept to themselves and minded their own business. Or did they?

Electra's business *was* other people's business. She was the surveillance genius, the information assassin who, for a select and very well-heeled body of customers, could find out just about anything. No piece of information was too taboo, too restricted or too arcane for her to find and retrieve. Electra depended on smarts and intuition to succeed in a dangerous world. Like most geniuses, she was a free spirit who preferred to live in her own world and by her own rules.

Electra took her coffee cup and made her way to the living room, Pearl dutifully trotting along behind her. No human soul other than Electra had ever set foot in the room – which was a good thing as she would have had a certain amount of trouble explaining away her rather peculiar decor. The entire living room had been given over to her hobby and, therefore, resembled the control room of a two-bit television studio, something on a par with, or maybe a little above public access cable. Television sets of various sizes, makes and quality were arranged in a semicircle around the same overstuffed armchair in which Pearl had been so memorably photographed. Electrical cables and bundles of fiber-optic wire snaked across the floor or were crudely duct-taped to the walls. Some of them disappeared into rough holes punched in the floor; others ran up into the ceiling and hung down like vines in the jungle.

Electra settled in her chair, grabbed a remote and clicked on a compact disc player, soft music filling the room. She hit another button and all four television sets came on. The first two showed completely silent, static interiors, nothing more than empty apartments. Nothing doing there. On the third was a wide-angle, overhead shot viewing down – an old woman rolling out dough for a pie crust.

'Yummy,' said Electra. She knew the woman. Her name was Mrs Sidney and she was Electra's downstairs neighbor. She was a nice old bird, but to a hard-core voyeur like Electra an old lady baking a pie left a lot to be desired.

The fourth television set showed the apartment directly above. This was the apartment of a young couple, Jennifer and Bob. Electra had a nodding acquaintance with them when she met the couple on the stairs, but she knew the most intimate secrets of their lives. She believed that they actually loved each other, but that the pressures of their everyday life – sex, money, family – put a strain on their relationship that was difficult to bear. They argued ceaselessly, a constant grind of carping and fault finding that went around and around, with nothing ever solved or resolved.

They were already at it, even at that early hour, and their morning spat showed every prospect of turning into a full-scale fight.

'Well, my mother says—'

Bob was glowering, sullen and sour, and cut her off. 'I don't give a shit what your mother thinks,' he said nastily. 'I'm not sleeping with your mother, I'm sleeping with you.'

Jennifer came back quickly. 'You won't be for long with that attitude.' She ran her fingers through her hair and looked at the ceiling. 'Honey, I don't know what to *do*. She puts so much pressure on me. She never lets up.'

Electra leaned forward and turned up the volume, anxious not to miss a word of the tragedy unfolding on the screen.

'Jesus, Jennifer,' said Bob angrily, 'if you're so worried about your mother's approval, why don't you move back home so she can pat you on the head every time she decides you've done something right.'

'Jerk,' Electra spat. She could tell that his words had cut Jennifer deeply. She always found herself siding with Jennifer during these little episodes, not just out of sexual solidarity, but because she did actually tend to think that Bob was being unreasonable. He never seemed to take the time to try and understand Jennifer's point of view. Their lives had to be lived his way, according to his rules – no dissent or protest allowed.

Jennifer started to say something, but suddenly words seemed so pointless. Tears welled up in her eyes and she fought desperately to keep herself from crying, but her sorrow overwhelmed her resolve. Electra's pager sounded, but she ignored it, so caught up was she in Jennifer's misery.

Bob was unmoved by her distress. He folded his arms across his chest and regarded her critically.

'Oh, good,' he said, a derisive smirk on his face. 'That's really good. Go ahead and cry if you want.'

Jennifer couldn't face him anymore. She ran from the room, seeking sanctuary in their small bedroom. The door banged behind her as she went and this seemed to annoy Bob more than anything that had happened that morning.

'You like to slam doors?' he shouted after her. 'Well, I can slam doors too.' He stomped to the front door, walked out and slammed the door so hard Electra did not need a microphone to pick it up – she could hear the noise through the walls, and the impact seemed to make the building shake.

Electra clicked another button on her remote and all four monitors changed pictures – each one a different angle on Jennifer. She reached out and brushed her fingers softly against the image. In moments like that she was more than a voyeur. She cared about the lives of the people she watched.

Her pager beeped insistently again, and reluctantly she turned away from the television sets, switching them off, leaving Jennifer alone in her anguish.

Electra moved to her desk, picked up a cellular phone and punched a number into the keypad. As she waited for a connection, she slipped a voice filter over the mouthpiece and picked up a stopwatch. There was silence for a moment and then a woman answered. Electra clicked the stopwatch to start it, meticulously timing her call.

'Room one fifteen,' the woman said.

'I have the merchandise,' Electra said. Instead of the light, silvery tones of her own voice, her words came out in a deep, masculine baritone. As she spoke, she fingered a computer disc on the desk. This was the merchandise.

The woman knew exactly what Electra was talking about. 'The buyers arrive at noon,' she said briskly. 'They're on flight ten fifty-five from Schipol-Amsterdam.'

Electra covered the mouthpiece of the phone and thought out loud. 'Off the plane. Customs and immigration – they're Dutch, no problem there . . . Half an hour.'

Before returning to her call, she made an adjustment in the voice-altering filter. 'I'll attempt contact at twelve-thirty p.m. and every fifteen minutes after that.' Her voice was high-pitched, like that of a five-year-old girl.

'You have the hard copy images?' the contact asked.

Electra nodded to herself and pulled a series of pictures from a brown manila envelope. The pictures were different from those that Rath had – but they showed the same set of faces. Electra studied the leader's image closely.

'Affirmative,' said Electra. 'What do I call the principal?' She glanced at the stopwatch. The call had lasted forty-eight seconds. She was going to have to break off soon.

'Call him Remy,' said the woman. 'How will they know—'

At fifty-five seconds Electra terminated the connection. Even in this day of super-computers and high-speed communications gear, tracing a phone call still required at least a minute of uptime. Electra was never on the phone for that long.

'They'll know who I am,' said Electra to Pearl. 'I'll make sure of it.'

It didn't take long for her to get ready. She packed up her equipment in a large duffel bag, and coaxed Pearl into her Porta Pet carrying case. A moment later she was in her convertible Mustang, driving to her appointment.

Chapter Eight

———————◆———————

Electra arrived at the downtown Hyatt about thirty minutes later, but bypassed the main entrance and turned left into the parking garage underneath the hotel. She gunned the sleek little car down the concrete ramp, pulled into an empty parking spot right up front and handed the attendant a crisp new twenty-dollar bill.

'You got it, lady.'

Electra flashed him a smile and carried her two bags for the elevators. She had taken the precaution of preregistering so she could go directly to her room, unseen by reception desk clerks or porters. The elevator stopped at the lobby to take on a couple of passengers. A man and a woman stepped into the car, the woman clad in a white sable fur coat which Electra estimated was worth something like twenty-five thousand dollars. But not for long...

The couple backed Electra into a corner of the elevator, a veritable wall of fur right in her face. She put down the Porta Pet, reached into her duffle and pulled out a small aerosol canister – it looked like a can of breath spray – but it wasn't. Electra shook the container and then applied a nice, bright red circle of paint with an angry slash through it.

The couple left the elevator completely unaware of Electra's covert act of vandalism. She looked down and winked at Pearl, who peered through the Plexiglas window, mewing plaintively.

'That was for you, Pearl.'

'Meow,' said Pearl.

'You're welcome.'

Remy, Electra's Dutch 'principal' – the buyer of her very expensive information – disembarked from the flight from Amsterdam and strode through the Seattle-Tacoma airport like a man in a hurry. Behind him his three subordinates fanned out like escorts – which they were, three brawny Dutchmen each dressed in an expensive leather jacket. One of them carried the only luggage the band required. And an expensive briefcase, which contained four state-of-the-art silenced 9-millimeter handguns and a fat brick of cash, the whole stash carefully smuggled through a half a dozen security points in Holland as well as a couple in the United States. They did not carry a change of clothes, no toothbrushes ... They weren't planning on staying more than a few hours.

This little brigade, Remy at the fore, was like a flying wedge, slicing through the crowds of travelers who thronged the concourse. The four men eyed the people as if expecting one of them to approach. They knew that they would be contacted, but they didn't know how or by whom.

Back at the Hyatt, installed now in room 718, Electra

had logged on to the Sea-Tac computer net and discovered that KLM flight 1055 had arrived. She smiled to herself and picked up the phone and dialed . . .

The soft voice in the airport public address system came to life and announced: 'Mr Remy, to the white courtesy phone, please. Mr Remy.'

Remy and his henchmen were jammed up onto a crowded elevator when the name came over the public address. The four men exchanged glances and then started pounding down the metal steps, snaking between people, stepping over luggage that had been set down and actually pushing people out of the way.

Angry travelers stared after the four men, but no one wanted to argue with any one of them – never mind their considerable brawn, the looks on their faces suggested that these were not men to be trifled with in any way, shape or form.

Remy pounced on the nearest phone while the three bruisers circled around him, taking positions as if they expected a shoot-out right there in the main terminal building.

'Hello? Remy here.'

Electra got right to the point. 'Are you ready to go shopping on the Home Information Network?' she asked. 'Because if you are, the price is forty thousand.'

The price was of no interest to Remy. 'Where are you?' he whispered.

'Are you ready?' Electra pressed. 'Yes or no?'

Remy nodded. 'Yes.'

'There's a pay phone bank in the Hyatt Hotel – just to the left of the main elevators,' she said, her words clipped. 'You have twenty minutes.' Electra broke the connection abruptly and clicked her stopwatch into life.

Remy glanced at his own, expensive wristwatch, nodded to his associates, and the four of them took off, racing for the exits.

Watching them go, buried back in the press of people, faceless, anonymous, almost unseen, was a lone man much interested in the movements of the Dutchmen. They were almost out of sight before he broke from the crowd and started following, scanning faces around him as he moved – there might be a rear guard planted in the airport, but he couldn't see it if it was indeed there. He followed skillfully, deftly, without any superfluous movement. He was Robert Rath.

The Dutch swept through the automatic doors and headed toward a limo. The driver was leaning against the front fender holding a hand-lettered sign. It read: 'Remy & Party.' The hulking Dutchmen piled into the back and the car moved off, stop-and-going through airport exit traffic.

Rath was just about to follow when he noticed a young man hunched over a bank cash machine. There was something about the cut of his flashy suit and his slick black hair that reminded Rath of ... Miguel Bain. Gun in hand, Rath pounced on the fellow and spun him round, the gun going straight into the young man's face. But it wasn't Bain's.

He had a handful of money that he had just withdrawn. His eyes were wide with fear. 'Here, here,' he stammered. 'Take it! Take it!'

In a move worthy of an old-fashioned Western gunslinger, the gun vanished back into the holster and Rath relaxed his grip. 'Sorry,' he muttered. 'Mistake. Sorry.' Rath hurried away shaken – and realizing that he was more jumpy on this job than he had been in years.

Electra was working quickly in her room at the hotel. Pearl watched with little curiosity – her mistress was always doing *something* a little out of the ordinary – as Electra lay flat on her stomach on the floor, unscrewing the air conditioning grate from the wall. She popped out the screen, revealing a vertical duct. She carefully taped a piece of heavy-duty cardboard inside the ventilation shaft, angled in such a way as to redirect into the room any object that might be dropped down from above. That done, she stood, dusted off her knees and checked her stopwatch. Eighteen minutes had passed since she spoke to Remy. If everything were running according to plan, then the limousine should be pulling up at the hotel in a matter of minutes. She grabbed a pair of binoculars and went to the window to scan the street below her. Right on time, the big car turned on to the street and pulled in at the main entrance of the hotel.

The men within did not bother to wait for the hotel doormen to open the doors of the car, but jumped out quickly, every one of them, to a man, looking at his wristwatch.

Electra counted. 'One, two, three, four...' She homed in on Remy. He looked tough and businesslike, but his three colleagues looked a little dim-witted, more muscle than brain. Electra appreciated that. Things were always a lot easier if you were dealing with a single leader. She turned from the window and reached for the phone.

The public phone downstairs in the lobby was ringing when Remy stepped up to it. He grabbed it on the second ring.

'Hello?' He looked around the busy lobby as his escorts

shielded him. Not one of them spotted Rath, who, that moment, walked through the front doors of the hotel.

'Pick up the Yellow Pages,' Electra ordered.

Remy did as he was told. 'Now what?'

'Lonely?' she said playfully. 'Are you in town on business? No one would ever know if you checked out the escorts ... Go on, give it a try.'

Remy flipped through the pages quickly and discovered, nestled in the pages of the escort advertisements, a stiff piece of cardboard, the only marking on it a magnetic stripe. It was an electronic room key.

'It's room nine-four-two,' said Electra. 'I want all four of you in there ... I don't want anyone circulating, trying to find out where I am. All four of you in one place – no deal otherwise. Got it?'

Remy nodded. 'Got it.'

'And if there's more of you, you can be sure I'll know about it. Understand? If I smell a rat, I go. Are we simpatico on that?'

'Yes,' said Remy. 'Simpatico.'

'I'll be in touch,' said Electra. She hung up.

Remy motioned to the three others and they walked straight into the elevator. Rath wanted to follow, but he couldn't without raising a red flag to the Dutch. As he watched the doors close, an overall-clad maintenance worker walked by. Rath had an idea ...

The elevator traveled one floor, to the mezzanine of the hotel, then stopped. All four of the men grumbled in guttural Dutch at the interruption of their ascent. The doors swept open and a pleasant-looking young man entered. He smiled and nodded. Miguel Bain was nothing if not polite. He pressed the button on the board and then took his place next to Remy. People in elevators don't, as a rule, talk to one another – and no one did now. Instead, all five of them did what strangers always do in elevators – they stared fixedly at the little lights illuminating their progress up through the building.

Just before the elevator stopped at nine, Miguel, as deft as a pickpocket, slipped something into the side of Remy's jacket. The instant the Dutchmen exited the elevator and Bain was alone, the smile on his face vanished, to be replaced with a grim frown. That was his business face.

Rath was working his own way into the action, but in a more roundabout style. He pulled out his cellular phone and dialed a number. The number answered immediately.

'Maintenance...'

'Yes,' said Rath. 'There's no electricity on the twelfth floor. None. The whole floor is completely dead.'

'What?' said the maintenance worker. 'Jeez. Sounds like we got a short in the switching box. I'll go straight up there.' The janitor dropped the phone, grabbed a toolbox and dashed out of the office.

A moment later Rath stole into the room and sat down next to the Datahost Hotel computer terminal. He had used this trick before in hotels all over the world. Datahost was the most common hotel computer management system and he knew his way around it well. He quickly pulled up the guest list, subtracted the vacant rooms from the total inventory, then deducted the blocks of rooms set aside for weddings, three conventions and the Chicago Bulls, who were in town to play the Supersonics. In one of the remaining rooms was his mark. Now he just had to figure out which one...

* * *

The Dutchmen entered their room, guns at the ready, and found it empty. There was, however, plenty of evidence that someone – Electra – had already visited the place and set it up according to her requirements. On the desk was a Phillips head screwdriver, a laptop computer hooked to a cellular phone modem and a remote intercom matching the one in Electra's two floors below. Remy glanced at the computer and noted, with great pleasure, that the screen of the laptop was set up for transmitting. This was going to be fast and quiet. He liked that.

She could hear the men blundering into the room. 'Close the door,' Electra ordered. The door banged shut.

'Okay,' she said briskly. 'First I need a ten thousand dollar deposit, just to make sure that we understand each other.'

'That wasn't in the agreement.'

By way of reply, the transmit codes on the screen of the laptop computer vanished and the machine clicked off.

'We have nothing more to discuss,' Electra announced. 'Good-bye.'

'Wait! Wait!' said Remy frantically. 'Okay. Ten thousand dollars.'

The computer came back on and whirred as it booted up again. 'Okay,' said Electra. 'Here is the menu for today.'

The screen filled with file names. Remy scanned down them and nodded. Everything was in order. He slid a disc into the A drive of the computer and waited for instructions on what to do next.

A faint beeping sounded, but it wasn't coming from

any of the electronic equipment on the desk. Rather, it seemed to be emanating from behind the wall of the room itself. The four men listened, guns drawn, wondering just what the hell was going on.

Electra was quick to enlighten them. 'I believe you'll find a screwdriver on the desk. Please pick it up and unscrew the screen from the air conditioning vent in the wall.'

Remy pointed to one of his men and signaled to him to do as Electra had instructed. Cautiously, with all the wariness of a man set to disarm a powerful bomb, the man took the screwdriver in hand.

He removed the four screws and pulled away the screen. Inside the duct stood Electra's little remote-control toy dump truck, a flashlight and a pen-size camera taped to the roof.

The Dutchmen exchanged puzzled looks. 'Now what?' said Remy.

Rath had narrowed his search down to three individuals. 'Clark, Rogers and Katz,' he whispered. Both Clark and Rogers were identified with the hotel code mm, which stood for Mr and Mrs. K. Katz, by contrast, had nothing before his or her name, but there were two rooms registered to that name, 718 and 942. On 942 there were no charges – no room service, no cable movies, no phone calls, no wake-up call – nothing. On 718 there were charges, the same thing over and over again.

'Coffee. Coffee. Coffee. Tuna fish. Tuna fish. Tuna fish,' Rath read. There was a note on the room service page that the tuna fish was to be platter only – not sandwiches. 'Tuna fish,' Rath said, thinking it over.

Then he reached into his pocket and pulled out and

unfolded the printout of the green cat eyes sent to him by The Contractor. Meow®comsat.net.

'Meow . . .' Rath whispered.

Chapter Nine

———◆◆◆———

Electra had become pretty proficient with the dump truck remote control. Watching the thoroughfare – the track of the ventilation system – on the tiny Sony television set, she guided back toward her the little vehicle bearing its ten-thousand-dollar cargo in the bed. It turned at one branch, hummed along and then turned left at another. Dead ahead was a square hole which dropped three stories straight down into the heart of the building. The truck rolled on, the front wheels almost at the edge of the abyss. Electra stopped right there, backed the truck into a perfect three-point turn that any examiner at all Department of Motor Vehicles would have been proud of, and then reversed the toy up to the lip. She punched a button on her remote and the bed of the truck upended, dumping the money into the hole.

The money fell two stories, hit the cardboard flange that Electra had installed in the duct and thumped onto the thick carpet of the room. Pearl jumped and scowled at this sudden intrusion, but Electra smiled. She grabbed the bundle and hefted it in her hand. It felt like ten thousand dollars. She riffled the edge of the notes with the tip of her thumb – it looked like it was all there.

'Have the next payment ready,' she said. 'I am about to go ahead and format your disc. You should orient it to receive data.' Electra started to type rapidly, sending the data through the network and into the hard drive of the machine in room 942.

Rath entered the elevator in the subbasement and hit a number on the board, feeling a little jolt of excitement, that same tingling sensation that he always felt when an operation shifted into high gear. Right then, Miguel Bain was the furthest thing from his mind.

Bain walked down the long corridor of the ninth floor, resolute, but excited about what was going to happen next. Near the elevators was a couch, a couple of armchairs and a credenza holding an elaborate floral display. Bain was surprised to see a couple, a young man and woman, sprawled on the couch, entwined and kissing passionately. It was as if they had gotten off the elevator and were so desperate to get their hands on each other they couldn't even wait to get to their room. They didn't care who saw them.

Bain walked by, smirked at them ... Then stopped, wheeled and fired twice, two muffled shots which struck both people square in the head. The couple toppled to the floor. Bain grabbed them both by the collar and dragged them into a stairwell. There, in private, he searched them thoroughly. Both of them were armed with silencer-fitted 9-millimeter handguns. He shook his head, as if to clear it.

'What the hell is going on here?' he said aloud. Then he shrugged. He didn't really care. Returning to the hallway, Bain stationed himself about halfway down along its length, pulled a cellular phone from his pocket, dialed up his beeper number and hit Send.

From one of the rooms came a loud beeping as the pager activated. Silently, Bain sprinted toward the origin of the sound.

Remy pulled the beeper out of his pocket – the one that Bain had planted on him in the elevator – and stared at it, a puzzled look on his face.

'A beeper?' he said. 'I don't carry a beeper.'

At that moment, Bain came smashing through the door of the room. He held his .22 in one hand and one of the 9-millimeters in the other. Both weapons were spitting bullets. Two of the escorts dropped before they could pull their weapons. The one remaining managed to get off a shot that went wide and embedded itself in the wall. Bain put three bullets into him before the hapless man had time to squeeze off another shot.

He iced Remy last, an artistic little takeout. Two .9s to the heart, two .22s to the head. It was all over in under eight seconds.

The intercom picked up the odd noises from the room above, the thwapping sounds of silenced slugs and the grunts of the men who took them. It was immediately obvious to Electra that something was going very, very wrong up there. She took her hands off the computer keyboard as if the keys had suddenly become hot coals.

Bain was busy checking the pockets of the men he had

just finished gunning down. All four carried badges. He knew the insignia very well. 'Interpol?' He had just murdered four agents of the International Police Agency. Bain sighed. 'Well,' he whispered, 'no time to worry about it now . . .' He looked at the four corpses sprawled on the carpet, their blood oozing and pooling on the floor.

'No more worries, my friends,' said Bain, as if he was saying a prayer. '*Suena con los angelitos.*'

Electra's voice on the intercom suddenly brought him back to the moment. 'What's going on up there?'

Bain looked at the intercom and the laptop computer. He could tell in a single glance that the information on the screen was far from complete.

'Hello?' said Electra. 'You still there?'

Bain cleared his throat and did his best to sound Dutch. 'Please complete the transmission,' he said.

'Who is that?' she asked, her voice plainly full of misgiving. Electra was flustered. Either it was her imagination or Remy was suddenly speaking with a subdued but nonetheless distinct Spanish accent. Whatever was going on, Electra knew she had to get out of there in a hurry. She had ten thousand dollars in hand – she would have to take a thirty-thousand-dollar loss on this job. At least she'd be getting out with her life and anonymity intact.

For once Bain was flummoxed – he was not quite sure what to do next. Electra heard no answers, so she began to erase the information on Remy's computer screen, her fingers flying over her own laptop keyboard.

Bain saw the information disappearing line by line and he fell on the machine, frantically trying to save some of it. But Electra had set the two machines up in slave and driver format – and she controlled the driver. The computer on the ninth floor would do exactly what she told it to.

Bain swore. 'I'm going to tear your heart out,' he spat. 'I mean it.'

Fear suddenly washed over Electra. She shut down the computer system and slung it in the duffel bag along with the essential equipment – she didn't bother with the intercom. That was an off-the-shelf item at any electronics store. Although she was in a hurry, she didn't forget the money. Unfortunately, she was forced to waste precious seconds chasing Pearl, who didn't really feel like getting in the Porta Pet right at that moment.

'Pearl! Dammit! We have to get out of here,' Electra whispered. 'Please, honey...'

Pearl finally gave in to Electra's entreaties and allowed herself to be captured and placed in the carrier. She thrust on her sunglasses. *Now* she could get the hell out of there.

But as she turned toward the door, it burst open and Electra found herself staring at the business end of a fat silencer attached to a .22-caliber pistol. Rath was almost as surprised as Electra. He had not expected to encounter a woman on this job.

Electra, for her part, thought that this dark and dangerous-looking man was the one she had heard on the intercom. Somehow, miraculously, he had tracked her down in a couple of minutes. She looked into his eyes and tried to stare him down.

'Don't,' she said. 'Please don't.' She was quite surprised to hear that her voice was steady, almost calm.

Bain's voice came through the intercom. 'Don't what?' he asked. Rath grimaced when he heard Bain's voice –

another job of his and Bain was there too. Now it was his turn to wonder what was going on.

Electra couldn't take her eyes off Rath and glanced at the intercom speaker. 'Who's that?' she asked no one in particular.

Suddenly, the situation came clear to Bain. 'Hey, Rath! Is that you down there?' He actually sounded pleased that Rath had shown up on this job. He had to find out where they were. Bain grabbed the television remote control and clicked on the set. He laughed. 'It *is* you, isn't it? Hey, small world, no?'

Rath ignored Bain's taunting voice. He held the gun steady in his right hand, aimed square on Electra, and reached out with his left. 'The disc,' he whispered. 'Give me the disc. Now.'

Electra nodded and thrust a trembling hand into her duffel and pulled out the disc. Rath took it from her and stowed it in a pocket.

Bain had opened the hotel's in-room check-out system, viewing the billing records for room 942 right there on the television screen. 'Hey, Rath,' said Bain. 'Did you check out that chess move I gave you? You did, didn't you? Black queen to king's bishop four?'

Bain was getting under Rath's skin. He stood stock still, his only movement a microscopic tightening of his finger on the trigger. The Contractor had specified that the surveillance expert be hit as part and parcel of the package. The men in 718 were gone. All he had to do was kill the woman and collect two million and quietly steal away into a blessed, but well-financed, obscurity.

But something stopped him. She was frozen, rigid with pure, unadulterated terror. She was no killer. That much was clear.

Bain's voice came through the speaker again. 'You got a move for me, Rath? Gonna play the game with me, the way you did with Nicolai?' He had gone through the file on the television screen item by item. All it showed was a lot of tuna fish and coffee, and that told him nothing. 'This is just like chess. What's your move? Is she alive? Did you kill her? Are you there, sweetie?'

Electra opened her mouth to say something, but she found she couldn't get out a word. Rath reached out and took the sunglasses from her face. She blinked at him, as if he had shined a bright light in her eyes. A tear escaped and streaked down her cheek.

'Is she dead yet, Rath? I took care of business on my end. What about you? Come on. Pull the trigger. *Kill her.*'

In the ninth-floor room, Bain had discovered something interesting. All that tuna fish and coffee had been charged to another room, 718. The account for 942 was yoked to 718. Well, if Rath wasn't going to ice the Meow lady, then he would have to do it. Silently he slipped from the room and ran for the service stairs.

It didn't take him more than twenty seconds to race down the two flights of stairs, sprint along the corridor and slam through the door of 718. The room was empty except for the pieces of the intercom speaker which Rath had blown away with a single shot.

Electra and Rath emerged from the elevator and entered the gloom of the parking garage. She was carrying her duffel and Porta Pet while he held her arm tightly, his .22 pistol wedged hard against her ribs.

'Where's your car?' Rath asked.

'I ... I don't know,' she stammered.

The attendant in the garage remembered the pretty

woman who had given him that twenty dollar bill. 'There it is, ma'am,' he said, eager to be of help. He pointed out the bright red Mustang. 'You said keep it close and that's what I did.' He handed over the keys and beamed. If he was expecting another tip, he was going to be disappointed.

Rath looked at the flashy car. 'I guess a black Chevy would have stuck out too much,' he said. The car was noticeable, but it was all they had and it would have to do.

Electra was just calm enough to drive, Rath riding shotgun, gazing back at the hotel, on the lookout for any trouble. There was no sign of Bain. She could drive the car, but she was still very nervous and very scared. And when she was nervous, she talked.

'I always thought I was going to die in a bus crash,' she said quickly. 'Isn't it dumb to think like that? I mean, the odds on getting killed in a bus crash are like five hundred million to one. You know what the odds are of meeting a stranger who is a killer? Not good. One thousand to one.'

Still holding the gun on her, Rath just stared. Electra tittered apprehensively. 'I guess I've been worrying about the wrong statistic. Isn't that stupid?'

Rath exhaled heavily. 'Relax,' he said wearily. 'If I was going to kill you, you'd be dead already.'

Electra hit the gas a little harder. 'Happy thought,' she said.

Chapter Ten

———◆◆◆———

Methodically, but with a high degree of destructive-ness, Bain tore apart room 718. He opened every drawer, turned over the mattress, slit it open and checked the insides. He tore up the carpet and dismantled the furniture, but try as he might he could not locate that computer disc. Bain sat down in the wreckage of the room and wondered how he was going to find that damn woman. Then he spotted Electra's computer case stuck in a corner and her jacket, both forgotten in her haste to get out of there.

The computer case yielded nothing, but in the pocket of the jacket he turned up the packet of photographs. He flipped through them quickly, looking at them with little interest. 'A cat,' he said in disgust. 'Cat outside, cat inside, cat sleeping ... Shit...' He tossed them away like a deck of cards and stood. He would have to think of something else. Then he stopped himself, squatted down and picked up one of the pictures.

It was Pearl outside, but that wasn't the thing that

interested him. It was the object behind the cat that caught his eye. The three huge transmit towers...

'Now, those would be hard to hide,' he said. Bain threw himself at the window of the room, sweeping aside the drapes and staring out over the city. He scanned the horizon intently. Then he smiled. There, in the distance, were the towers.

'Back in business,' he whispered.

Electra had gotten rid of enough fear and replaced it with anger. 'Who the hell are you anyway?' she demanded. She took her eyes off the road just long enough to shoot Rath a furious glance.

'I work for the government,' said Rath simply.

Electra downshifted and sped up. 'Bullshit,' she snapped. 'And where the hell are we going, anyway?'

'Just drive,' Rath ordered. 'Okay?'

'You want drive?' she said. 'I'll give you drive.' Electra hit the gas hard. The Mustang bucked and leaped forward. The needle on the speedometer sailed past forty, then fifty, and was well on its way to sixty. Rath hardly noticed. He dug Electra's laptop computer from her duffel and plugged his cellular phone into the machine. He typed in The Contractor's number and the system came on-line in a matter of seconds.

The Contractor: *This is not a scheduled call, Robert*. He could almost hear the maternal clucking from The Contractor.

Electra was doing over sixty, but she was in pretty heavy traffic so she was forced to weave through the stream of cars, like a downhill skier on a slalom course. Rath looked up from the computer.

'Would you watch your speed, please?'

Rath typed: *He was there again.*

The Contractor: *Shut down. We'll talk at the scheduled time.* Rath's computer died as The Contractor broke the connection.

'Slow down!' Rath had to shout to be heard over the rushing wind and the roar of the powerful five-liter engine.

'I can't.'

Rath reached over with his left foot and pushed it down on the brake, and the car lurched and slowed considerably.

'So what about the other guy?' Electra asked. 'Does he work for the government too?'

Rath shot her a nasty look and pulled his foot off the brake. 'What do you think?'

'I don't know what to think,' she said angrily. 'All I know is what I heard. All that stuff about chess. This is some kind of game between you and whoever that guy is. Well, I don't care. Just leave me out of it.'

'We can't,' said Rath.

'Why not?'

'Because you're part of it.'

Electra did a double take. 'Me? Part of this? How can I be part of this?'

'You're the mark,' Rath said simply.

Electra was silent for the next five minutes, driving sedately now, turning over this new information in her mind. It didn't take her long to figure out what she had to do: escape. She had to grab Pearl and abscond. And she had to do it quick before she had two killers looking for her.

They were approaching an intersection and Electra touched the brake, slowing down for a moment. She glanced at Rath, braced herself in her seat and then jammed down on the accelerator. The car raced forward and rear-ended the pickup truck in front of them. Electra knew the crash was coming and was ready, but it took Rath totally by surprise. His head slammed into the dashboard, cracking him hard across the forehead.

Electra saw her chance. Rath was stunned long enough for her to grab the Porta Pet from the backseat and take off. She dashed down the street, crossing over through a thicket of traffic. Sneaking a glance over her shoulder, she saw Rath getting out of the car and running after her.

'Dammit!' she whispered. Up ahead a bus stood at its stop taking on the last of a line of passengers. She tried to pick up the pace, looking back once again – then she slammed smack into a man walking down the sidewalk minding his own business. The Porta Pet fell from her hand and rolled end-over-end down the pavement.

Rath was gaining, closing the gap between them. There was just no time for Electra to retrieve her pet. She was acting on survival instincts alone, throwing herself onto the bus. The doors hissed shut and the bus lumbered away, leaving Rath flat-footed on the sidewalk, staring after it.

Electra hurried to the back of the bus and peered out the wide rear window. She got there just in time to see Rath stooping to pick up the Porta Pet.

'Oh, Pearl,' she whispered. 'I'm so sorry...' Electra slumped down in a seat. She had escaped, but at what cost?

Rath walked back to the Mustang, the Porta Pet in his hand. An irate motorist, the man whom Electra had rear-ended, was capering around his smashed pickup, shouting something about car insurance. He was silenced instantly by the wad of bank notes Rath thrust into his hand.

'Shuttup,' he said, as he climbed back into the Mustang. He drove a few hundred yards and then pulled over to search the car thoroughly. There was nothing in the trunk or glove compartment that gave a clue to Electra's address. The only thing of any use at all was a paper bag with a few grains of cat food inside. But the food came from a 'gourmet' pet food shop. The name of the store was Prize Pets and it was on Auburn Avenue.

It turned out that Pearl was something of a big shot at Prize Pets. The elderly woman behind the counter recognized her immediately. 'Pearl! How are you, dear?' She looked doubtfully at Rath. 'Pearlie, where is Mama?'

'I was wondering the same thing,' Rath said affably. 'I found this cat along with a bag of food from your store. I was wondering if you could let me know how to get in touch with the owner.'

'I'll take her,' said the pet shop owner. 'I'll see that Pearl gets home safe and sound.'

'Well, I was kind of hoping...'

The woman knew the score. This man had found the cat and he wanted a reward. That seemed fair, if mercenary. He had gone to a lot of trouble, after all. 'I'll check the order book,' she said. 'I might have an address...'

* * *

Bob returned home to Jennifer late that afternoon feeling sick at heart; he hated himself for the harsh words he had inflicted on her that morning and he wanted nothing more than to take his girl in his arms and apologize for being such a brute.

Bob got out of his car, and hanging his head, he walked into his building, hoping that Jennifer was still there. Somewhere in the pit of his stomach, he had the sickening idea that she had gone home to her mother. Bob walked a little faster . . .

Bain walked up to the building a few moments later, going from car to car, feeling the hoods to see which was still warm. Bob's was the most recent arrival. Bain noted the apartment number on the parking place and smiled to himself. Then he walked into the building.

Electra was in her apartment, packing as fast as she could. She was throwing stuff into her duffel without rhyme or reason. The monitors were on in the living room, but she didn't even glance at them. Rather, she circled the room throwing objects into the bag – a book here, a sheaf of papers there – then she headed for the bedroom to retrieve as much of her wardrobe as she could carry.

Bain slipped the woefully inadequate lock on Bob and Jennifer's apartment door in a matter of seconds. He stepped inside and made directly for the living room. He made little attempt to muffle his footsteps – he was going to kill the woman anyway – and he wanted to find the disc as quickly as possible.

Bob heard footsteps coming down the hall and walked toward them. 'Jenn?' he called.

No answer.

Shit, he thought, she's still mad at me ...

'Jenn, I love you.'

Bain was right there, filling the doorway. 'That's so sweet,' he said.

Electra had everything she needed, or everything she could grab in five minutes. She slung the bag over her shoulder and walked out of the bedroom. She went to shut off the monitors and saw the terrifying scene unfolding in the apartment below.

'Who are you?' Bob looked alarmed.

'You'll never know ... Romeo.' He raised his gun and backed Bob into a walk-in closet. Electra hadn't wired the closet for pictures or sound, but her microphone did pick up the muffed retort of the gun and the sound of Bob's lifeless body falling to the floor.

The killing did not seem to bother Bain in the slightest. When Bain reappeared on the monitor, he had a small, self-satisfied smile on his face. He stopped in the middle of the room and seemed to take the whole place in with a single glance.

The look on his face changed as he glanced up at the smoke detector set in the ceiling. Bain was trained to look for bugs and cameras, and the first place you ever checked was in light fixtures and ... smoke detectors.

Electra's mouth was open in horror as Bain's face suddenly loomed huge in the monitor as he looked directly into the camera. He was standing on the bed, peering at the plastic housing of the monitor. His hand reached up to it, his mitt giant on the screen. Then the picture rocked crazily as he yanked the plastic box from its moorings.

Bain's warped little smile came back as he looked at the mini camera hidden where the test button should have been.

'You sick little bitch.' He whispered the words, but she could hear him loud and clear. He seemed to be speaking directly to her, as if he knew she was listening.

Chapter Eleven

———◆◆◆———

Her heart racing, her throat so dry she thought it would close up and suffocate her, Electra turned to leave. But she stopped dead in her tracks when she heard a sound in the hallway beyond the living room. It was the wistful meowing of her cat. A moment later, Pearl trotted into the room, Rath right behind her.

Electra let out a little cry of relief and scooped her beloved cat up in her arms. Now she could disappear without so much as a backward glance at her own life. She didn't know where she was going to go or what she was going to do when she got there ... But as long as she had Pearl, she could put up with anything.

Rath drew his gun from his holster, cocking his chin at the monitor. Bain was still there.

'Where is he?'

Electra pointed to the floor. 'Downstairs.'

Taking Electra by the wrist, Rath pulled her out of the apartment. They snuck downstairs and out into the street. He put the woman and her cat in the Mustang.

'Wait for me at the pet shop,' he ordered. 'Understand?'

She nodded, slammed the car into gear and pulled out, smoke pinwheeling off the fat rear tires as she roared away. She was amazed to be alive.

Rath was back in the building a moment later, leading with the .22, as if the snout of the weapon could sense danger ahead. Moving stealthily, he opened the door of Jennifer's apartment – Bain had not bothered to lock it – and crept down the hallway, making for the bedroom.

No Bain. Rath looked up at the wires dangling from the ceiling, then over at Bob's legs which were poking out of the walk-in closet. As he knelt to take Bob's pulse, he heard the tap-tap-tap of footsteps on the ceiling above. Someone was in Electra's apartment. It could only be Bain.

Electra had managed to calm her hammering heart a little bit and her driving was slightly more sedate as she made her way down the hill. Pausing at a stop sign, she buried her head in her hands and breathed deeply.

The horn in the car behind her blared, urging her to get along. 'Okay, okay,' Electra muttered. As she started off again, she passed a car going up the hill, a car that looked vaguely familiar. Electra cried out in horror when she realized that it was Jennifer heading home after a day at work.

'No!' Electra yelled. 'No! Jennifer! Don't go back there!'

But Jennifer didn't hear her, driving by, blissfully unaware of the troubles that lay just seconds ahead in the future.

Electra couldn't let that happen. She jammed her car

into reverse and backed up fast, nearly smacking into the car coming up behind her. The angry scream of a horn ripped through the evening air and a man leaned out of his window.

'Jesus Christ! Where the hell did you learn to drive? Get the fuck off the road before you kill someone!'

Electra didn't bother to answer. She wrenched back on the shift, slammed the car into gear, hopped the curb, crossed the median and slammed down on the highway going back up the hill, driving as fast as she dared.

Both Bain and Rath were in Electra's apartment now, but only Rath knew it. Bain was in the bedroom, burrowing through the dresser drawers so recently rifled by Electra herself. He paused for a moment and picked up a bottle of Electra's favorite perfume. Pulling out the glass stopper, he held the vial to his nose and sniffed deeply. 'Ahhhh,' he said, closing his eyes. 'Jasmine...'

Bain almost jumped out of his skin when he opened his eyes. Rath was framed in the mirror of the dresser, right in front of Bain's eyes. He recovered in an instant, whipping around like a piece of sprung steel, firing rapidly. Three bullets slammed into Rath, but he didn't go down – he shattered. Bain had blasted away the full-length mirror screwed to the back of the bedroom door.

Bain guessed at where Rath was and fired, blasting slugs through the thin plaster walls. Rath ran, just steps ahead of the line of bullets which burst from the wall behind him. He dove into the kitchen. He looked up and saw a pipe snaking across the ceiling, and following it with his eyes, he saw that it terminated in the stove. It gave him an idea that should take out Bain once and for all.

Bain, for his part, was far from done. He slapped a fresh clip into the gun and jumped from his cover, the barrel of the gun sweeping across the open space. Rath was in the kitchen, Bain could sense it.

'You're getting slow, *Abuelo*,' Bain yelled, breaking the silence.

Rath answered: 'I'm not the one shooting at mirrors.'

One floor below, Jennifer walked into her apartment. Her heart sank when she discovered that the door was open. She had been hoping that Bob wouldn't have returned home yet. She wanted a moment or two of peace and quiet before he came in and the wrangling began all over again.

But if the door was open, Bob was somewhere within. With a resigned sigh, she walked down the hall and into the bedroom. Her eyes went directly to the jumble of wires dangling from the ceiling and to the pile of dirty plaster on her nice clean bed. She did not see Bob's body.

Angrily she turned on her heel and strode out of the room. 'Bob?' she shouted. 'Where are you?'

She threw open the door to every room in the apartment, but couldn't find her boyfriend. In desperation, she mounted the stairs toward Electra's apartment, hoping that she had some idea of what had happened here.

Unfortunately, she made the mistake of walking in on Bain. Sadly, it was the last mistake she would ever make.

'Who the hell are you?' she demanded. Then she saw the gun in the man's hand. She paled and her eyes seemed to flood with fear.

'The disc,' he said, holding out his hand. 'Give me the disc.'

Jennifer was frozen for a moment – then she bolted for the door. Bain dropped her before she had managed a step, killing her with a single shot to the back of the head. Then he whipped around and faced the kitchen.

'I beat you to the buyers and now I beat you to the mark,' Bain shouted. 'I'm starting to think I picked the wrong guy to be my hero.'

Bain waited for a moment, hoping he had goaded Rath into making a response. The slightest sound and he had him nailed. He tuned his ears to the silence, ignoring the sound of a Mustang screeching to a halt in the street outside. Rath's answer did not come, so Bain decided to try again.

'You know, Rath, you should be congratulating me...' Bain laughed. 'That's right. 'Cause today's my birthday. It's true. Today I become number one.'

Bain reached down and picked up a large shard of the shattered mirror and began inching his way toward the kitchen door. Bain tossed the piece of mirror into the kitchen, the large scrap breaking up into a dozen smaller fragments. One of them fell and leaned against the wax, angling inward so that Bain could get a good look into the room, almost a full view. He couldn't see Rath anywhere.

'You got a present for me, Rath?'

Bain felt tense now as he began to edge into the kitchen. There was another doorway in the far corner of the kitchen, the door through which Rath had made his escape. There was a trail of liquid on the floor leading out the door, but Bain paid no attention to it.

He slumped against the sturdy oak kitchen table, his shoulders drooping. He couldn't quite bring himself to believe that Robert Rath would actually run away from Miguel Bain. But the facts were the facts. He really *had* chosen the hero, though he hadn't believed it until that very moment ...

Then he sniffed the air. It wasn't jasmine he smelled; this time it was the sickening smell of gas.

In that very moment, he heard the distinctive sound of a match being struck. Then the liquid on the floor – it was brandy – ignited and the flame raced out from under the door.

'Make a wish,' Rath shouted. He turned and ran down the stairs, meeting Electra on her way up. There was no time for words. He tackled her around the waist and dragged her down.

The gas ignited a split second later.

Chapter Twelve

---◆◆◆---

Bain had about a second to try to save his life.

As the flame zipped into the room, he upended the kitchen table and dove behind it. The tremendous detonation rocked the building to its foundations, and in the instant the air ignited around him, Bain felt as if he had been picked up and pitched across the room by some huge and powerful invisible hand. The table, his only protection, was blown backward as if it were as light as a leaf, then caught fire like a pile of dry kindling. Bain, who had never been in the middle of an explosion before, felt like a cork bobbing on furious waters hurtled backward, the lick of the flames searing the clothes off his back and catapulting him through the window in a ball of fire and burning debris.

Electra felt as if she had died and gone to hell. Even with Rath's body on top of her, protecting her from the worst of the blast, she could feel the heavy blanket of heat rush through the stairwell, the building shaking so violently that she was sure it was going to collapse around them like a house of cards. As the blast wave subsided, the air was filled with a number of different smells and sounds. The air was heavy with the odor of barbecued meat, singed hair, burning pain, caustic smoke. Every car alarm in a five-block grid had been set off, the electronic wails and howls filling the air like an assembled band of banshees.

And yet, it was all over so quickly. In less than a quarter of a second, the gas had burned itself out. There were still some residual flames burning in the kitchen – mere brushfires compared with the big blast – and the hallway was filled, floor to ceiling, with hot, biting smoke.

Rath was the first to move, rolling off Electra, coughing to the depths of his lungs, like a smoker with a bad hack. He got wearily to his feet as Electra picked herself up, coughing and gagging, tears streaming from her eyes.

'You stay here,' Rath said, his voice hoarse, giving her no time to reply or protest as he climbed the stairs, vanishing into the haze.

There were a few flames still burning in the kitchen but there wasn't much left to burn – most anything that could be set on fire had been incinerated in the first blast. Bain was gone, of course, and Rath glanced out the window hoping to see body parts scattered around. There was a lot of debris scattered on the backyard lawn, but nothing immediately identifiable as human.

Jennifer's body, still sprawled in the hallway beyond the kitchen, seemed to have been unharmed by the blast. Rath went to her and checked for a pulse, but he could tell by looking at the vicious head wound that this was a futile gesture. He was sickened by the death of this woman and her man, unwitting pawns in a deadly game. They would never know why they had died these pointless and meaningless deaths.

Feeling as if he had a piece of lead in the place where his heart used to be, Rath returned to Electra. She was still crouched on the stairs, stunned into a dazed silence.

'Come on,' he said.

'Wait,' she said. 'We have to find Jennifer.'

He shook his head. 'I'm sorry,' he said softly. He turned her gently and led her outside to the car. Electra was amazed to find that the world still existed beyond the charred ruin of the apartment building, that normal life seemed to be going on as before. It seemed unreal somehow, artificial. As if to reassure herself that she had returned to the real world, the first thing she did was gather Pearl up in her arms and hold her close.

Sirens were wailing, as fire engines hurried to the scene.

'We have to go,' he said. Electra did not appear to have heard. She continued to clutch her cat, staring at the wreckage of her house. She could not obliterate the thought of the two bodies that lay within the charred rubble, two lives snuffed out in an instant, two people who on awaking that morning had not known that this was their last day on earth.

Electra was still alive, but it had been a long, harrowing, terrifying day and she felt herself withdrawing from the world, closing herself off from all the pain and terror she had witnessed in just a few short hours. Rath had seen this kind of shock before; he had seen it in the eyes of soldiers after their first fire-fight – he knew there was nothing he could say, no words that could soothe the pain or erase the images from the mind. So he just shut up and drove.

There was no better temporary hideout than a character-less, nondescript chain motel on a commercial strip just off the interstate. Rath chose one such establishment at random, driving into the forecourt, registering with the listless, indifferent night clerk, then ushering Electra to the drab little room.

Weary but still wary, she entered the room but she looked worried, as if she suspected that the place had been set with a half a dozen lethal booby traps or thought that the moment she crossed over the threshold the killing would begin all over again.

It took a few minutes for her to reassure herself that she was safe, but she felt like a prisoner in a cell nonetheless.

Electra sat on the edge of a vinyl-covered armchair, Pearl in her lap, and watched as Rath gazed out of the window, memorizing every feature of the commonplace highway-scape beyond the door. Then he drew the curtains and prowled the room, checking every drawer and looking under the bed. Electra was amazed to see him take hold of the telephone, dismantle it, check it for bugs and then put it back together again. The world she lived in was uncertain, the game she played was danger-ous, but she imagined that it was child's play compared to his.

Rath removed his jacket. Electra stared hard at the webbing of the holster and the dull, weighty gleam of the handle of the .22. He stripped off the rig, wrapped the belt around the holster and set it down on the chipped and scarred coffee table. She found it hard not to look at the gun, her gaze following the weapon the way a dog eyes a tempting treat.

Rath dropped onto the beat-up sofa, exhaled and rubbed his eyes. It was the first time that day that he had relaxed.

Abruptly, Pearl climbed down from Electra's lap, stretched voluptuously and then padded across the shag toward him.

To Electra this was plainly an act of treason. 'Pearl,' she ordered brusquely, 'come back here.'

Pearl, however, had every reason to trust Rath. It was he, after all, who had rescued her in the street and it was he who had reunited her with Electra. 'Pearl...?'

Pearl ignored her. She leaped up into Rath's lap, kneaded his thigh with her front paws and then settled there. Rath scratched her ears gently.

Angry and embarrassed, Electra felt her cheeks grow hot and she snapped her fingers, furious at this small act of betrayal. But Pearl paid no attention, settling further, closing her eyes and beginning to purr, contentment showing plain on her face.

Rath shrugged. 'She likes me.'

Electra glared back at him. 'She likes dead fish too.'

'So do I,' he said mildly. 'If prepared properly.'

As he looked down at the cat, Electra looked at the gun, estimating the distance from her chair to the weapon. She was pretty sure she could get to it before he stopped her – as long as she had surprise on her side. The first order of business was, therefore, to attempt to put him at ease.

'What do you call yourself?' she asked.

'Robert Rath,' he said.

She laughed. 'Oh, that's a good one. It really suits you.

Wrath? Like the wrath of God? Or the day of wrath ...
Dies Irae?'

'R-a-t-h,' he said, spelling it out for her. 'What do you
call yourself?'

'You can call me Electra...' They both knew that these
were not their real names. The need for anonymity in
their respective strange worlds was just part of doing
business. Electra had chosen her own name, a *nom de
guerre* that she thought suited her; she could not know
that Rath's name had been assigned to him by The
Contractor. She was silent for a long moment, then she
sighed, aware that her ability to chitchat someone into a
state of carelessness was not great. 'I'm not very good at
this sort of thing...' She rose from her seat and paced the
room nervously. 'I don't think I have much time,' she
said, 'so I'll just go ahead and get started.'

Rath watched her, looking amused.

'You are probably wondering what I'm thinking,' she
said. 'That's simple enough. I'm scared. I've almost been
killed twice in one day and I'm afraid the last time may be
the charm. That's the kind of thing that would bother any
normal person, wouldn't you say?'

Rath didn't answer; he just continued to watch her as
she walked back and forth. 'Furthermore,' she continued, 'if I don't get a cup of coffee soon, I'm going to
jump out of my skin. And last, but not least, I've been
kidnapped by a man who I suspect does a job you can't
find in the yellow pages. Am I right so far?'

Rath nodded. 'So far.'

'So you can see that my only option, the only thing I
can possibly do, is to try to escape.' She looked at him
pointedly, like a skilled debater scoring serious points.
'Do you see any other alternative here?'

As Rath looked down at Pearl, Electra lunged for the gun. She grabbed it and struggled for a moment to free it from the holster, then leveled it at Rath, half-scared by the power she held in her hands. Rath had not moved a muscle: he hadn't even blinked.

His unnatural calm unnerved her. 'What?' she asked. 'It's not loaded?'

'It's loaded,' he said. 'And silenced. You could shoot me right now and only Pearl would know. I think you can trust her to keep her mouth shut.'

'Don't think I won't,' she said through clenched teeth. 'I could be five hundred miles away by morning.'

'That's true,' Rath said, nodding.

Electra kept the gun on him, but she couldn't shake the feeling that he still, somehow, had the upper hand.

'You said you worked for the government. It's a guess but I have a feeling you don't work for the IRS ... I figure you must be one of ... them?'

'Them?' Rath asked. He seemed to be genuinely puzzled by her question. 'One of who?'

She shrugged, as if embarrassed by her own question. 'You know ... Like a spy or something. With the CIA ...'

'I used to be.' Rath glanced at his wrist-watch as if he were late for an appointment. 'I'm retired now.'

Electra looked unconvinced. 'Oh. Sure. Right.'

'If I was still what you think I am, you wouldn't be pointing that gun at me,' he said. He smiled. 'Would you?' Rath stroked the soft fur on Pearl's belly.

'Stop that,' Electra snapped. 'She doesn't like that.'

But Pearl increased the depth of her perfidy by purring even louder. It was the only sound in the room.

'What's the matter?' he asked calmly. 'Are you afraid that you'll hit the cat?'

Very gently, as if he were handling a fragile and delicate thing, he lifted Pearl and placed her on the floor. 'There...'

Pearl did not look pleased and, in that feline sense of self-importance, could not imagine what could be so significant, so meaningful to these two humans that they would have dared to disturb her ease. She sniffed haughtily and walked away, stretching and yawning, as if Electra and Rath were too boring for her to care about.

A look of stern determination crossed Electra's pretty face, but even she was astonished when her finger tightened on the trigger and she started squeezing off rounds. A bullet hit a lamp and the fixture exploded, showering Rath with fragments. Pearl jumped and hissed, her back arched in fear.

Two more bullets slammed into the couch, gouging out wispy tufts of cheap stuffing. Rath did not move.

'Sit down!' Electra ordered. She was flustered and afraid.

'I am sitting down,' said Rath calmly.

'Shut up!' She stepped forward, the gun aimed square at his chest. 'Now I'll tell you what you're thinking. You were thinking that I wasn't going to shoot you ... But now you're not so sure, are you?'

Rath had to admit to himself that she was correct. He was surprised that she had fired at all, and now he could not be a hundred percent positive that, blinded by the heat of her towering fury, she wouldn't put a bullet in him.

'You think letting me get this gun was a mistake, don't you?' Her voice was high and tortured: the combined weight of the terrible events of the day seemed to slam into her. 'You think maybe I'll do something irrational because I'm a woman and I'm freaked out, don't you? *Don't you!'*

She fired again, two more blasts, the round digging into the wall above his head. 'You don't know shit about me!' She took another step closer and aimed the gun at Rath's face. 'I want to know why you didn't kill me. Why am I alive? Huh?' Her voice turned low and sarcastic. 'What was it? Love at first sight?'

Rath sighed and shrugged. 'I couldn't shoot you then,' he said simply. 'You won't shoot me now.'

Electra's finger tightened on the trigger. Rath merely stared back at her, waiting to see what happened next. In a funny kind of way, he didn't really care what befell him, and he realized, for the first time, that he didn't mind the thought of dying. What bothered him was who killed him, actually pulled the trigger. The thought of dying at Bain's hands was repugnant to him and he would fight that to the very end. If his life were taken by this strange, lonely, beautiful young woman... He could live with that. A slight, bemused smile appeared on his lips.

This seemed to infuriate her. Electra's finger tightened on the trigger, her hands trembling terribly now, the gun barrel shaking. At this range, though, even with quivering hands she could not miss.

'Just let me go,' she said sadly. 'Please ... I don't have a social security number. I barely remember my real name. I'm a ghost. I can hide.'

Rath shook his head. 'I found you today. So did he. You can't hide.' It wasn't a threat; it was a simple statement of fact.

The words struck her harder than any bullet. She jerked to the left and fired a wild shot, blowing a cheap print off the wall. Lowering the gun to her side, she fought back tears, not protesting as Rath rose and eased the gun out of her hand.

'I need to be alone.' Electra sounded drained, exhausted. 'I haven't spent this much time with someone in years.'

The tears were almost there. Electra moved blindly for the bathroom. Pearl had returned to her original allegiance, dutifully following after her mistress.

'Neither have I...' said Rath as she closed the door. He sat in the shadows and listened to her sobs.

Chapter Thirteen

———◆———

If Electra's day had been bad, Miguel Bain's had been worse. He had been shot at, blown up – but worse than all that, he had failed. Bedraggled and unkempt, he wearily dragged himself into a phone booth, unscrewed the mouthpiece, hooked up his computer modem and logged on.

The Contractor was waiting for him. *What went wrong, Miguel?*

Bain: *Nothing went wrong. I retired the buyers. And the seller.*

The Contractor: *And the disc?*

Bain was taken aback by this response. He was not used to being criticized and he stared unblinking at the screen.

The Contractor then did something Bain had never known him to do. He repeated himself. *The disc, Bain. Where is the disc?*

Bain typed, feeling foolish for having to make excuses. *Rath has it. He's a difficult mark.*

The Contractor's response was so quick it was like a

stinging slap across Bain's face. *Rath is not the mark. THE DISC.*

Bain felt like a schoolboy called on the carpet by the principal. His reply was petulant and peevish. *You'll get it.*

A long, long pause followed – so long that Bain thought The Contractor had signed off. He typed the *are you there* command and was rewarded by a tight-lipped response: *Wait.* And he waited, almost a full two minutes of dead time. Bain grew jittery – not even The Contractor was this reticent.

Finally, the connection was resumed.

The Contractor: *The contract has been reassigned.*

Bain's mouth dropped open and he gaped at the words on the screen. 'What? No lo peudo creer!' He typed a single word: *Why?*

The Contractor: *You had your chance. You failed.*

Rage enveloped him. *Fuck you!*

The Contractor: *That's no way to talk to a lady.*

'I don't care what you are,' he shouted at the screen. He hit the repeat key and *fuck you* scrolled line after line on the display. In the middle of the cloud of obscenities The Contractor logged off. Frustration overcame Bain and he slammed his fist against the thick glass. He stared out into the night. He wanted revenge. Rath would pay . . .

It was Rath's turn to log on with The Contractor. Electra was still in the bathroom, but the crying had ceased, replaced with the pounding of water in the shower.

Rath: *I have the disc.*

The Contractor: *You're still the best, Robert.*

'Then who's the kid?' he muttered as he typed. *I want*

the two million in cash. This was not standard operating procedure. Payment for services rendered was usually made by electronic transfer to Rath's bank account in the islands.

But The Contractor seemed unconcerned by this unusual request. *Where do you want to make the trade?*

For once, Rath had the upper hand. *I'll let you know,* he typed and logged off.

When Electra emerged from the bathroom, Rath was seated in the armchair facing the television set. The late news was on and as he watched he toyed with the computer disc, turning it in his hand over and over again.

Electra watched over his shoulder. 'What did they say about the dead guys at the Hyatt?'

'Nothing.'

'I don't need details.' She wound a towel around her wet hair like a turban. 'Just in general. What did they say?'

'Nothing.'

Electra was taken aback. 'Absolutely nothing? It didn't make the news at all? Four dead men and it didn't get on the television news?'

He shook his head slowly. It didn't surprise him in the least, of course.

'What about Jennifer? And Bob?'

'Nothing,' Rath said again.

'The explosion? Did they mention that?'

This time Rath nodded. 'That they reported on. It was caused by a faulty gas line. No casualties. They called it a miracle.'

'Nothing on the Hyatt?' she repeated.

'How many times do I have to tell you? No, nothing.'

'That's just impossible.'

'No. It's not impossible. Not if ...'

'Not if what?' she demanded.

'Not if they were CIA,' Rath explained. 'Or Interpol.'

As the weather came on the news, Rath leaned forward and clicked off the television set. He considered the disc for a moment, then held it up.

'What's on this?' he asked.

Electra shrugged. 'I don't know. It's fully encrypted. I could break it on my laptop but it would take two, maybe three hundred years.'

Rath smiled. 'I thought you were a genius.'

'I am,' she said, returning his smile. 'In fact, I was the best at what I did.'

'*Was?*'

'I'm retiring too.'

'I don't blame you ...' He held up the disc again. 'But you have no idea about this thing.' Rath had his own hunch, but wondered if he really wanted to know. He was sure of one thing: this was more than the recipe for synthetic heroin.

'I wish I had an insight,' Electra said apologetically. 'But it was all anonymous. Just an intercepted satellite transmission. The cipher is rock solid. I've never seen anything as dense. You'd need a Kray at least to break it.'

Rath nodded. He understood that in this case ignorance was definitely bliss. It was probably a little safer too.

Electra was exhausted. She pulled down the bedspread and plumped the pillows. 'There's only one bed,' she said. 'But I guess you've already picked up on that.'

Rath retreated to the bathroom and returned a moment later, rolling two towels together, fashioning a makeshift pillow.

'The bed is all yours,' he said. 'Take it.' Rath set the roll down on the floor – but it wasn't a spot chosen at random. It was directly under the bright overhead light.

Electra watched. 'You don't want the couch?' she asked.

Rath shook his head 'No. The floor is better.'

'You're going to sleep with the light in your eyes?'

'That's right.'

'What is that? A trick of the trade? Making sure you don't get too comfortable?' She smirked at him, as if he were an overeager Boy Scout. 'Why don't you just tie a string from your toe to the doorknob? Then, if the door opens, you'll get a tug; you wake up and you can blow away all the bad guys. Neat, huh?'

Rath didn't have to think twice to find a defect in her plan. 'Wouldn't work,' he said quickly. 'The door opens in.'

As Electra slipped in between the sheets, she did something she hadn't done all day. She laughed. It was a nice sound.

Rath kicked off his shoes, set the .22 at his side and lay down, staring at the ceiling, trying to order his ideas, planning the day that lay a few short hours ahead. He had to get in touch with The Contractor and give him detailed plans for the exchange – they were only half-formed in his mind now. He also had to devise some strategy for getting Electra to safety. She knew nothing, but she was probably still a mark. The downside of eliminating Bain was that the new assassin would be anonymous and faceless.

Electra interrupted this train of thought. 'Thanks,' she said.

'For what?'

'I don't know,' she said softly. 'For saving my life, I guess.'

If she expected modesty or aww shucks humility, she did not get it. Instead he took her completely by surprise.

'How'd you like to make a million dollars?' he asked. He knew he needed her help to make the transfer – and a million dollars would be a small price to pay if the transaction could be pulled off without complication.

'What do I have to do?' she asked, amused.

'It might be dangerous.'

'Oh, that,' she said with a dismissive laugh. 'That's no problem ... I just won't do anything cheap. I hope you understand that...'

Chapter Fourteen

———————◆◆◆———————

Rath awoke before sunup, showered and dressed in the predawn gloom. By then Electra had roused herself. Fifteen minutes later they were in the Mustang searching for a diner open so early in the day.

They sat over coffee for more than hour, Electra drinking cup after cup as Rath carefully outlined the plan for the transfer. The plan was complicated, but the thing that seemed to worry him most was the amount of caffeine his partner was ingesting.

'Doesn't that make you jumpy?' he asked anxiously. 'You're going to have to keep your wits, you know.'

Electra shook her head. 'To the contrary,' she said. 'If I don't get enough of it, I get very, very cranky.'

'I've seen that side of you,' said Rath, smiling. 'Not a pretty picture. Particularly if you happen to have a gun in your hands.'

'Then you see what I mean...'

Zero hour was 10 a.m. Electra was behind the wheel of the Mustang, driving soberly along a busy downtown street. She wore her dark sunglasses and her hair was tucked into a kerchief – it was as close to a disguise as she could manage.

Rath pointed to a spot at the curb. 'Pull over there. Okay,' he said, as they rolled to a stop, 'follow the plan. And if I don't show, you know what you have to do.'

Electra nodded vigorously. 'I know, I know. I split.'

Rath barely nodded. Reassuring a woman was a subtle skill he had never mastered. He reached into the backseat and grabbed the laptop, then looked around for something he couldn't find.

Electra held up the disc. He reached for it, but she pulled back, like a kid playing keep-away.

'In ten minutes you'll have a bag containing two million dollars cash,' she said seriously. 'And you'll have no reason to come back. I tried to ditch you yesterday. I'm sorry about that, but I didn't know you all that well at the time. And who knows, maybe you hold it against me and—'

Rath interrupted the flood of words by placing his fingers gently against her lips, a gesture of absolute finality.

'Partners,' he said, as if swearing a solemn oath. 'Understand? We're partners.'

Electra nodded and handed over the disc. Rath got out of the car and Electra watched as he disappeared, swallowed up by the mid-morning crowd.

'Be careful,' she whispered. 'Partner...'

Rath stepped onto the monorail at Fourth Avenue and Pine, traveling north. He scanned the other passengers in the car, knowing as many as a dozen of them might be operatives working for The Contractor. He recognized no one.

Taking a seat, his back to the window, Rath turned on the computer and inserted the disc. Instantly, a long list of file names glowed on the screen, but they meant nothing to him. Most of all, he was happy to be getting rid of it.

A southbound train was entering the station as Rath's monorail pulled in, and the two trains stopped across the platform from each other. A man stepped from the train, a briefcase in his hand. Rath knew a courier when he saw one so he walked toward him. The two men met in the middle of the platform and the courier opened the briefcase a crack, displaying wads of bills – twenty stacks of thousand bills.

The transfer was made quickly, the briefcase exchanged for the laptop computer, the two returning to the trains and continuing on their way. Rath sat, the weight of the briefcase in his lap. He had to admit to himself that it felt good.

The Contractor had an observer on the train, a middle-aged man, sitting reading the paper, his back to Rath. But he could see Rath quite clearly, watching him closely, reflected in the discreet piece of mirror tape stuck to the inside of the frames of his thick horn-rimmed glasses.

Midway between stations, Rath made his move. He stood suddenly and, before anyone could react, yanked down on the handle of the emergency brake set in the ceiling. The monorail screeched to a halt, the passengers thrown forward in their seats.

Rath ran down the aisle and hit the panic button to open the door standing right at the edge, looking down. About twenty feet below him was the tar-paper roof of a commercial building – an easy drop. Rath didn't hesitate. Briefcase in hand, he jumped, landing and rolling on the roof.

The doors hissed closed and the observer, peering down, watched as Rath swung on to a fire escape and made his way to the ground. The whole getaway took less than a minute.

Rath could hear the Mustang before he saw it. Loud music, thundering rock and roll, was pouring from the powerful sound system, filling the street with noise. The car screeched to a halt in front of him. Rath jumped in and they were gone.

Electra glanced curiously at the briefcase. She had always been well paid for her specialized labors, but she had never come close to putting her hands on a million dollars all at once – never mind in cash.

'It's in there?' she asked.

Rath nodded. 'Every penny.'

'It's so . . . small.' She sounded the tiniest bit disappointed.

'Want to see?'

'Just a quick peek,' she said, a mischievous look on her face.

As he angled the briefcase toward her, the music on the radio cut out abruptly, replaced by a confused and chaotic burst of static. Rath frowned and moved the briefcase to his right – instantly the radio reception returned, the air full again of rock and roll.

The radio was cutting out because it was too close to a powerful transmitter. And a transmitter could mean only one thing – bomb.

'Turn left!' he ordered.

Electra cut directly into a lane of traffic and gunned the

engine, pushing the car straight down the dingy, deserted side street. Rath heaved the briefcase with all his might, throwing it as high as he could into the air. Twenty-five feet off the ground the bomb detonated with a tremendous blast and suddenly it was snowing shredded money.

Without thinking, Electra slammed on the brakes and gawked at the money that seemed to fill the air.

'Go!' Rath commanded.

'But ... But the money ...'

'Leave it. Go!'

Electra went. She roared down the street, turned right and took off. It wasn't until she was back in traffic that Rath spoke.

'No money,' he said glumly. 'And no disc either.'

Though profoundly shaken up, Electra did manage to smile, that knowing smirk that suggested that she was very pleased with herself. 'Well ...' she said philosophically. 'It's not so bad. Could be worse. Could be a lot worse ...'

'What?' said Rath. 'What are you talking about?'

'It's simple. I really wasn't sure you'd come back. This morning I switched discs.'

'But I checked,' he said incredulously. 'I saw the files.'

'Credit me with some intelligence,' she said sarcastically. 'I took out the files, but left the file names. That's all they got. A list of file names. In other words, bupkis.' She took one hand off the steering wheel, rummaged in her purse and pulled out another computer disc.

'This is the one they wanted. Instead they got nothing. Zero, a goose egg, jackstraw, nix, nada, zot, zilch, squirt, a dry hump, diddly-squat ...' She smiled sweetly. 'I read a slang dictionary once. From cover to cover.'

Rath nodded. 'Keep reading.'

'You know,' she said. 'I'm beginning to get the hang of this.'

'Really?'

'Yeah. Your contractor just tried to kill you.'

'That's right.'

'That's not good.'

Chapter Fifteen

Electra decided it was time for a little celebration and she did it in her own idiosyncratic way – by buying Pearl a present. She pulled into the parking lot of a gourmet shop and emerged a few moments later with a glass jar – a container of Osetra caviar.

She scooped out an oval of the glistening eggs and held it in front of Pearl's nose. The cat's pink tongue took a dainty little lick.

'Funny thing about caviar,' she said. 'It's sold by the pound, but there aren't sixteen ounces in a pound of caviar. Not sixteen, fourteen. In Russia before the revolution, a pound was fourteen ounces. When the Bolsheviks took power they decided they would leave things as they were – they brought in the metric system for everything, except caviar. I guess they figured that they would continue to shortchange the western imperialist running lackey pig-dogs. In the name of revolution.'

Rath glanced at her. 'Is that it? Are you finished?'

'No,' she said smiling brightly, 'there's more.'

'Great,' said Rath.

'Do you know,' said Electra, 'that caviar is not a Russian word? No one is really sure where it comes from. Could be French, could be Italian, maybe Turkish. But one thing is for sure, it's not Russian.'

Rath nodded. 'I know. In Russian it's called *ikra*.'

She regarded him critically, trying to fathom how he knew this. The look on his face told her that it wasn't just some stray fact he had picked up somewhere. It had a source that meant something to him.

'How did you know that?' she asked casually.

Rath opened the laptop and typed in the access code for The Contractor. 'I had a Russian friend. Nicolai. He told me.'

Electra raised an eyebrow. 'Had?'

'Fifteen years ago,' said Rath sadly. 'He was taken.'

'Killed?'

Rath nodded. But before Electra could delve any deeper, The Contractor came on the line.

The Contractor: *Robert, is that you?* He seemed very surprised to be hearing from him.

'That's right, you son of a bitch,' Rath growled at the screen. 'I'm still alive.'

Rath: *I still have the disc.*

The Contractor recovered his aplomb quickly. *We can make new arrangements.*

Rath could play it cool too. *The price has changed.*

Electra peered over his shoulder, watching as he typed. 'Let's see how valuable he thinks that damn thing is.' He typed a number two followed by a series of zeroes – a lot of zeroes.

'Twenty million dollars!' exclaimed Electra. 'But that's insane. I can't believe he'd ever go for that.'

'Insane?' said Rath. 'May well be. But let's see what he says.'

There was no activity on the screen. The Contractor was taking a moment to think things over.

'Where do you think this person is?' Electra mused aloud. 'Right now, where is he? A mile from here? Ten thousand miles?'

It was a question Rath had pondered for years, until he banished it from his mind for fear that it would drive him insane. 'I haven't thought about that for a long time. Not until now.'

Electra chuckled. 'Let's see now ... You quit your job, you fight with your boss, you're thinking new thoughts. Sounds like a midlife crisis to me.'

'Yes,' said Rath. 'And I think you're it.'

Suddenly The Contractor's answer slotted up on the screen. *Robert, agreed. It will take two days to arrange the transfer. What is the bank code and account number?*

Pulling a small leather-bound notebook from his pocket, Rath checked the long sequence of numbers and letters and typed it in.

'I don't believe it,' said Electra in amazement. 'Twenty million dollars and all he wants to know is your account number!' She was silent for a moment. 'By the way,' she asked innocently, 'are we still partners?'

Rath nodded.

Electra almost burst into tears. 'Ten million each!'

'Eight million,' Rath corrected. 'The bank will take twenty percent. For services rendered.'

Electra knew that twenty percent was a pretty hefty fee for a simple wire transfer – only very select and very shady banks would charge that much. 'Oh,' she said. 'It's that kind of bank?'

119

'That's right.' Rath started the car. 'Do you have a passport?'

'I have twelve,' she answered. 'Where are we going?'

'South,' he said.

Bain had recovered from his terrible day. The cockiness was back, there was a spring in his step and he had a brand new, shiny nugget of hate in his heart for Robert Rath. He drove himself to the airport, turned in his rental car and settled down with his laptop computer.

'Time to talk to the man,' he said, typing in The Contractor's contact code.

The Contractor: *Miguel? Are you there?*

Bain could tell in an instant that this was not the haughty, disdainful Contractor he had communicated with just the night before. There was a note of pleading in those words; he could hear them as clearly as if they had been spoken. Something had gone wrong. The Contractor had bid out the job on Rath and it had come unstuck. Bain was back in business.

He laughed and settled back, deciding to make The Contractor sweat a little bit.

The Contractor: *Miguel ... You know what I want.*

Bain paused and then typed in his single condition. It had nothing to do with money. It was about respect.

He typed: *Say please.*

There was a long, long pause. But then Bain watched with satisfaction as the letters appeared, slowly, grudgingly: *P L E A S E ...*

Chapter Sixteen

There was only one place on the face of the earth where the sea was this color. It was crystal clear yet at the same time shot through with the brilliance of intense aquamarine – it was a shade of shimmering blue that could only be the Caribbean.

The island itself was a small patch of dark green vegetation set in the middle of that wide silver-blue sea, a mere flyspeck of land. The population was small and, for the most part, impoverished. The vast majority of the people eked out a meager living working in the only labor-intensive industry on the island, tourism. A number of gleaming hotels lined the white beaches but the only locals in these vast pleasure palaces were gardeners, chambermaids, cooks, waiters and busboys, each one of them dependent on tips and the almighty dollar.

It was odd, then, that a small, poorly paid population should have required the service of so many banks. There were dozens of them, lining the main street, Camino Real, and they ringed the central square, Plaza

Colon. Some were discreet offices, air conditioned to an icy chill, their existence advertised by nothing more than a small brass plaque. Others were vast, old-fashioned temples of money, built to resemble stately homes, classical temples or the grand palaces of ancient and illustrious Spanish grandees.

A particularly astute observer could not have failed to notice the most peculiar aspect of the banking scene on the island. Although there were close to a hundred banks, not one of them had a name that would be recognized by the ordinary, average checking and savings account-holding citizen of the USA. There was no Chase Manhattan branch on the island, no Bank of America, no Fleet Bank, or Continental or Nation or Citibank.

All the banks on the island had names so bland that they meant almost nothing: Bank of Trade, Bank of Commerce, Banque du Commerce Internationale, Transnational Bank, Bank of Credit and Exchange...

But whatever the name and the size and luxury of the premises, all of these banks had several things in common. Business was never discussed in a voice louder than a circumspect whisper and actual legal names were rarely used. The bankers and their customers preferred a system of passwords and codes as well as the nice anonymity of numbers.

The most important thing that all these banks shared was the kind of money they dealt in. It was almost all, down to the last dollar, pound or Deutschmark, dirty. The island was a sunny place for shady money.

These financial institutions sheltered drug money, small streams of dollars from the streets of urban America which became a vast torrent of riches as they poured onto the island. There were millions of British pounds parked on the island to avoid the baleful stare of the Inland Revenue tax collectors back in the UK, money earned through the sale of weaponry to certain outlaw countries in the Middle East. There was Mafia money from Italy, money from the French criminal organization Union Course, cocaine money from a dozen Latin American countries, opium cash from Burma and a vast pool of filthy money from the new Russian Federation.

The island was a favored hiding place for slush funds and bribes, for payoffs and kickbacks for the nest eggs of dictators, huge deposits made by African despots and Asian tyrants, insurance against the day when their subjects rebelled or an upstart strongman forced them into making that last, inevitable helicopter flight from the roof of the Presidential Palace.

Robert Rath was only one of a thousand secret operatives who appreciated the guarded manner in which business was conducted on the island – he had maintained an account there for years.

He and Electra emerged from the plane at the airport, wincing as the heat hit them like a fist. Both wore sunglasses against the glare and appeared to be nothing more than two additional Yankee tourists coming to the island in search of sun, sea and frozen drinks in lurid colors.

But instead of joining the other holiday makers on the shuttle buses to the seaside hotels, Rath and Electra grabbed one of the beaten up, rattle-trap taxis waiting at the stand just beyond the main entrance of the airport.

'*Donde va?*' the taxi driver asked.

'Hotel Paradiso, *por favor*,' Rath replied. In response the taxi driver glanced in the mirror and gave him a strange look, but then sighed and shrugged and put his rust-bucket car into gear and pulled out.

As the car bounced over cobblestones, Electra looked out the window, taking in the luxuriant tropical vegetation and the dilapidated houses and shops that lined the highway. This was a side of the island that foreigners rarely saw. Most tourists made directly for their hotels and stayed in those compounds for their entire stay, sheltered and protected as if in a harem.

Rath looked straight ahead, unseeing. He had been there before and he seemed preoccupied with his memories. No one in the cab spoke until the car lurched to a halt in front of the Hotel Paradiso. The building was not as he remembered it. Fifteen years before it had been a slightly down at the heel establishment, its glory days behind it, but you could still see traces of its former elegance, like a faded dowager fallen upon hard times, but determined to keep up appearances.

Now the Paradiso was a blackened hulk; the walls once painted a dazzling white were stained with soot. The rafters of the roof had fallen in, the windows were smashed, the lush garden surrounding was trampled and untended. Fire had killed the old building, dealing a swift death blow, rather than the slow demise brought on by the international tourist trade.

Rath was shocked. 'The Paradiso? What happened here?'

The cabdriver spoke slowly in thick, heavily accented English. 'Fire, señor,' he said. 'Two, three months ago.'

Rath got out of the car and stared up at the hotel, his eyes settling on the blackened window on the third floor.

That day so many years ago came rushing back, the power of his memories sharp and intense like an electric shock.

He swung around and looked at the bank, tracing a line from the hotel to the front steps. In his mind he could see the swirl of pigeons, he could hear the sounds of the market ... He could see the body of his mark sprawled on the cobblestones, dead of a single shot to the heart. Rath could see the man's face: Nicolai Tachlinkov.

Electra's gaze settled not on the burned-out hotel but on the International Bank across the Plaza Colon. It was a beautiful old building, the ornate black iron bars on the windows contrasting with the vivid white of the bleached, whitewashed walls.

'Is that the bank?' Electra asked. 'Is that where our sixteen million is?'

But Rath wasn't listening; his mind was miles away in the past. She followed his gaze to the third-story window. Electra glanced at him, slightly spooked by the odd look on his face.

'What's up there?' she asked. Then, suddenly, she wasn't sure she wanted to know.

'Right now?' said Rath. 'Nothing...'

'There's a big fat But in there somewhere,' said Electra. 'What'll be there tomorrow?'

'He'll be there.'

Despite the extreme heat, Electra shivered. 'You think he'll try to shoot you when you go into the bank?' she asked.

Rath shook his head curtly. 'No. Not when I go in ... When I come out.' He spoke as if the coming events were established by edict and chiseled in stone.

'How can you be so sure?'

'Because I was once at the same window. Fifteen years ago.'

'Fifteen years ago...?' And then, suddenly, everything came clear to Electra. 'Oh my God,' she whispered. Rath turned and looked at her, but his eyes were hidden behind the lenses of the dark glasses.

'Your friend,' she said. 'Your friend Nicolai. You said he was ... *taken.*' Electra's head swam. 'You killed him.'

Rath nodded. 'That's right.' It was hard for him to say those words, to confess out loud the wrongdoing he had kept in his thoughts for all these years.

Suddenly she was scared – very scared, as if all the things that had happened already were just an overture to a terrible final act that would be played out on the stage of the Plaza Colon. She looked at him for a moment, then put on her sunglasses, as if the thin discs of glass would protect her, as if the less she saw the more secure she would be.

Like every other foreigner on the island, Electra and Rath ended up at one of the luxurious tourist hotels on the coast. It was a tall, rambling complex of buildings set on a bluff with views of both the ocean and the city itself.

As they entered the opulent lobby, they did their best to blend in, to look like all the happy holidaymakers who had come to the island to forget the cares of their real lives back home.

Electra could smile, but Rath found it hard going. The reception desk clerk who checked them in was pretty sure he knew the score. Not all the men and women who came to the island were happy and carefree. Once in a while a couple checked in who had arrived here to 'work on their relationship,' hoping that a few days away from the pressures and stresses of kids and jobs and family would work as some kind of healing balm, soothing the hurts in an injured marriage. The clerk fit these two guests into this category. The man was grim faced and the woman was traveling with her cat – that was always a bad sign.

As they followed the bellboy across the foyer and up the steps to their room, they passed a young couple. They were holding hands and giggling like teenage sweethearts. It was obvious that they were a pair of newlyweds, a man and woman just a day into their marriage.

Suddenly the two of them stopped, right in the middle of the walk, and started kissing passionately. Rath paid no attention to them, but Electra couldn't tear her eyes away, envying the love and the passion they so plainly felt for each other.

As Electra and Rath reached the room, the newlyweds came stumbling up the stairs behind them. Not only were they quartered on the same floor as Electra and Rath, they were in the room right next door. As the bellboy opened the door, the lovers fumbled with their key. Electra lingered in the doorway. The woman could not keep her hands off the man – literally. Electra watched hungrily as the woman ran her hands passionately over her new husband's chest and whispered and sniggered in his ear. He finally managed to open the door and the couple tumbled into the room. It was obvious what they were going to do next.

Electra entered her own room and put her ear to the wall. Sounds of laughter could be heard, but that quickly gave way to passion.

'You should check them out,' said Electra, smirking. 'Maybe they're Interpol or CIA or something.'

She couldn't know that Rath had already considered that possibility and had rejected it. He was in no mood to fool around. 'They're not,' he said. 'Not even professionals could pull off an act like that.'

The sounds from the other side of the wall became more intense and Electra couldn't resist grabbing a glass from the minibar and holding it to the wall. She rested her ear against it, a makeshift stethoscope.

Rath watched her, distaste showing plainly on his face. The elaborate monitoring system in her apartment or a glass against the wall, Electra was a hard-core case. 'You're a voyeur,' he said with disgust. 'You watch instead of doing.'

Electra heard the repugnance in his voice and glared at him. 'There are worse things to be,' she snapped at him. Her own words were filled with as much revulsion as his.

Rath was stung, but he knew that she spoke the truth. Electra had gotten hold of a piece of him, possessing a bit of knowledge she could not understand. But she couldn't forget it either.

He tried to explain. 'Look,' he said, 'Nicolai and me—' Then he could not explain the inexplicable. 'It's none of your business.'

'It *is* my business,' she said fiercely. 'I'm with you!'

Rath had decided that he would say no more, but Electra could not let the matter drop. Passion was building on the other side of the wall; she wanted to listen but this was more important. 'I can't trust you,' she said. 'You can't trust me. How can we possibly help each other?'

'I trust you.'

'Why?' Electra demanded. 'Why do you trust me?'

But Rath didn't have an answer and looked away. Electra shook her head slowly, then she stooped and scooped up Pearl, retreating to the bathroom. Rath could hear the snap as the lock latched firmly.

Chapter Seventeen

———◆———

Bain walked across the Plaza Colon at dusk, relishing every step, like an actor on a stage feeling the excitement and thrill of an approaching first night. He looked at the bank and at the hotel – just as Rath had done – and felt impatient for the dawning of the new day. Rath had won too many rounds, had stayed alive too long. Tomorrow all accounts would be settled, the last round of the last bout would be played out. Bain planned to win by a knockout.

The market was closing for the night, the vendors breaking down their crude stalls and stowing away unsold merchandise. Bain decided that he needed a little snack. He crossed the square quickly and stopped the last stall holder before he could close up.

'*Un momento, por favor.*' The vendor sighed and waited stoically as Bain ran his eyes over the fruit. Each piece was examined carefully, as if Bain were looking at gemstones in a jeweler's case. After some time he finally chose two apricots.

'*Quanto es?*'

'*Diez centavos*,' said the fruit seller. Ten cents...

Bain was in the mood to be generous. He took out his wallet and handed the shopkeeper a crisp twenty dollar bill. '*Tenga*,' he said.

The fruit vendor had barely made twenty dollars all day; to be paid so handsomely for two apricots ... He looked at the bank note and then at Bain. There was something in the look in Bain's eye that told the vendor to pocket the bill and shut up.

'*Graçias, señor*,' he said, his eyes down.

'*De nada*...' Bain ambled away. He bit into the apricot, his mouth filling with the soft, sweet flesh, savoring the taste. As he chewed slowly, he gazed at the bank, looking at the big black iron gates that barred the front door. There was something almost medieval about the weight and thickness of the bars, as if all one had to do to be secure was to gird oneself with enough iron. But Bain was a perceptive observer – beyond the old gates he could just make out the steady red light of a sophisticated security system.

Bain took another bite from his apricot, then swung around and looked at the Hotel Paradiso. In the half-light of dusk, the burned-out building looked even gloomier than before. It was the natural place to shoot from and, by instinct, Bain's eyes settled on the same window from which Rath had shot fifteen years before.

Bain imagined the sight line, tracing an imaginary line from the hotel window through the air across the Plaza Colon to the main door of the bank. He finished the first apricot and spat out the stone. He didn't eat the second one. Rather, he placed it on a column ledge just to the right of the entrance to the bank and then walked away. He crossed the plaza to the hotel, pulling aside some boards haphazardly nailed across the old front door. Stepping inside, he picked his way through the debris and stood in the middle of what had once been an atrium. The roof had collapsed and he could look straight up and see the darkening blue of the night sky and the shimmering disc of a new moon. It cast enough light to make a fretwork of shadows, patches of black and white, on the floor and walls. Bain walked slowly through the ruin and he seemed almost reverent, as if this were a place he held holy.

Slowly, testing its timber as he went, he started up the stairs, cautiously making his way to the third floor. He traveled the length of the wrecked hallway and entered room 302. As he walked into the room, a floorboard gave way beneath him, his leg disappearing into a black hole as far as mid-shin. Bain braced himself against the soot-smeared wall and pulled his leg out of the cavity. He walked across the room to the window.

He could see the bank clearly and the vertical angle was not too extreme. There was no doubt in his mind that if he drew a bead on Rath, he would be able to drop him with a single shot. He unzipped his bag quickly, and with a minimum of movement assembled his sniper's rifle, screwing the two-foot-long silencer onto the end of the barrel. The gun nestled against his shoulder, he closed one eye, sighted the crosshair of the scope on the front door of the bank and squeezed the trigger. The hammer clicked home and Bain smiled. It was as good as over. Now all he had to do was wait...

Electra had come out of the bathroom but it seemed that she could not stand to be in the same room as

Rath. She passed straight through the bedroom and walked out to the balcony. Electra breathed in the lush, moist air and gazed down at the city spread out at her feet.

Something caught her eye. A procession was moving slowly down a cobblestone street. It was a long crowd of adults and children. The men carried lanterns, the women strew flower petals on the stones and the children capered about, each one of them painted with crude white lines, face covered by a ghoulish skeleton mask. They seemed to be making their way toward a cemetery that stood on the edge of town.

There was a knock at the door and Rath tensed. The .22 pistol was in his hand in an instant and he held it at the door.

'Who is it?'

'Room service.'

Rath leveled the gun. It was just about the oldest trick in the book, but it worked more often than one might have expected.

'I didn't order room service.' He cocked the trigger and started to open the door.

Just then Electra stepped in off the balcony. 'I ordered it,' she said.

Rath pulled the gun away from the door and paused a moment to collect himself, breathing in sharply and letting it out slowly. Then he holstered the gun and opened the door.

The waiter smiled diffidently and rolled in a cart spread with a number of covered dishes. He busied himself setting up the leaves of the table and laying out the cutlery.

'Excuse me,' Electra said. 'What is happening out

there?' She gestured toward the balcony and the procession beyond.

'The Day of the Dead, señora,' said the waiter.

'What does it mean? What are the flowers for?'

'Families make a path from their homes to the cemetery,' the man explained. 'So the souls of the dead loved ones can find their way back to their homes.'

'That's fascinating.'

The waiter smiled and handed the room service check to Rath. He signed it, adding a hefty tip.

'Can we go?' Electra asked. 'Can we go take a look at the procession?'

Rath waited until the waiter had left the room before replying. He shook his head. 'No,' he said curtly.

'Why not?'

'Because it's not safe. He'll be here by now. We stay in this room tonight and go to the bank tomorrow morning. That's it. Understand?'

Electra looked disappointed. 'Is it safe to watch from the balcony or do you think he'll pick me off?' she asked sarcastically. 'Maybe we should just turn out the lights and lie on the floor.'

Rath was tired of her harangues. 'Why don't you just go out on the balcony?' he suggested wearily.

Rath wondered how it was that she resented so much his efforts to keep her alive. It wasn't as if she hadn't seen the havoc and death that Bain could bring about. He sighed and hoped that the next twenty-four hours would pass quickly. He was getting tired of fighting a war on two fronts.

'I think I will.' She poured herself a glass of wine from the carafe on the table, grabbed a plate of food and vanished through the sliding door.

Rath poured himself a drink too, but it was something stronger than white wine. He dug a small bottle of scotch out of the mini bar and emptied it into a glass. As he sipped, he noticed what had never been there before – a slight tremble of his hand. The pressure was beginning to get to him and that was bad. One more day – that's all he had to do. He had to stay at the top of his game for twenty-four hours and he was free.

It wasn't that he was afraid of Bain – far from it. He was tired and sick of his world. Furthermore, returning to the scene of his greatest crime had stirred up a lot of old feelings – these he was afraid of.

After a moment, he set down his glass – the alcohol would not settle his nerves as well as confusion would. He stepped to the open balcony door and spoke through the gauzy drapes.

'I wish I could explain why I killed Nicolai,' he said, speaking into the darkness. 'I may have been manipulated. I don't know ... But for what it's worth, I'm sorry I did it.'

He waited for a moment, expecting her to say something, to forgive him. But she was silent and he couldn't really blame her for her reticence.

'I used to hope that the same thing would happen to me,' he continued. 'At least it would have been a way out.'

She remained silent, but this time Rath stepped out onto the balcony to be with her. 'Electra?'

The balcony was empty. Alarm pounding through him, he leaned over the railing and searched the ground below. She wasn't down there either. Electra had climbed down the fire escape and disappeared.

Chapter Eighteen

The procession emerged from a tunnel and advanced toward the old gates of the cemetery, the route lined with spectators, many of them American tourists from the big hotels. No one looked twice at Electra; all eyes were focused on the throng of people. The night was lit by the soft platinum glow of a thousand candles scattered through the graveyard, and the air was filled with marigold petals like a golden, sweet-smelling snow.

Electra stood next to two old women, one selling thick, sweet strong coffee from a giant thermos, the other dispensing brightly colored shaved ice. The swirls of light and darkness, the faces of the children and their parents – all this enchanted Electra. The procession had broken up within the cemetery itself as each clan made its way to the family plot. The gravestones were old and cracked. Some were elaborately carved and worked, sprinkled with angels and crucifixes and the beatific faces of the saved. Other headstones stood at crazy angles, having rocked to one side as the earth had warped and buckled over the years; some had toppled over completely and lay flat on the ground.

Electra's eyes were bright with enchantment. She loved standing in the dark secretly observing others – and this ceremony was prime people watching.

She felt that special thrill she always got when she was secretly observing her fellow human beings. There was nothing she would rather do. She was almost an anthropologist, watching and remembering, as if she was studying some obscure and remote tribe. Fading into the woodwork – or the dark – came naturally to her. Electra could vanish, sliding into camouflage like a chameleon.

'*Hola*,' said a voice. '*Que pasa?*' Bain had approached the two women selling coffee and ices and smiled a friendly smile. He was about four feet from Electra and she could not take her eyes off him. He did not acknowledge her, his eyes fixed on the people in the burial ground. But when he spoke, he spoke in English.

'Death is like me,' he said. 'Quiet, but a little scary. Sharp too – he's real sharp. And even though you want to stay away from him, you can't. He draws you to him. You dig him and fear him at the same time...'

Electra heard the words and felt fear grip her. There was something about his voice and words that unnerved her. Could this handsome young man with the ready smile be the man who had come to kill Rath?

'It's like me,' Bain continued. 'I am a million years old, but I look like I'm thirty...'

Electra could not stand the tension. She hurried away into the darkness, running among the tombstones. Under her breath, she cursed herself for having escaped from the hotel, exposing herself to danger. She was running now, rushing through the night, spooked. She did not know where she was going; all she knew was she had to get away.

Her foot caught on a prone headstone and she fell, sending an old glass candle holder flying. She could hear the tinkle of broken glass in the darkness as the candle holder hit the earth and smashed.

Bain heard it too. Instinct took over. He reached into the inside pocket of his jacket as he headed into the darkness. The two women vendors watched him go, then they exchanged glances, the coffee seller making a little circle around her temple with her fingers.

'*Loco*,' she said.

The other woman nodded vigorously. '*Es la verdad*,' she agreed. Neither of them thought much of the young man – the Day of the Dead, they knew, had a strange influence on some people.

Electra hid behind a statue of an angel, sure that the sound of her heavy breathing would give away her hiding place. She was convinced that she was being hunted, that there was someone out there in the darkness ... Him. He was there somewhere and he wanted her.

Bain stepped up and looked around. All of his senses were working, including smell. He sniffed the air deeply and smiled. He had smelled that scent before.

'Jasmine,' he whispered under his breath.

Electra slowly uncurled from her crouch and stood, moving backward, away from the statue of the angel. She had only traveled a step when a hand closed over her mouth. She felt a bolt of fear shoot through her. It was as sharp as a blade and it seemed to slice her in two.

Slowly she was turned around and in the faint light she looked into the eyes of her abductor. Then the sweet warmth of relief flooded through her. She was looking into the face of Robert Rath...

Bain was getting a little spooked himself. Sure that he had cornered someone, he darted around a row of tombstones, his gun aimed. But the space was empty. Looking about in the dark, he could feel the sense of capture begin to fade away – but there was still that scent of jasmine in the air. Then he spotted it, a bunch of white flowering jasmine standing in a vase before a tombstone. Rath chuckled to himself and shook his head, amazed that he had allowed himself to get unsettled like that. That just wasn't like him. In common with Robert Rath, he would be happy when this operation was finally at an end.

Miguel Bain did not know it, but his fear should have been real. Rath had spotted Bain and brought up the gun, taking aim in the darkness, ready to take him out. As Rath drew a bead on his target, a knot of mourners crossed between the two men. There was no shot. When the people had cleared out of the way, Bain had moved on.

The last game of cat and mouse would have to play out on the chessboard of the Plaza Colon, as if it had been predestined.

By the time Rath and Electra returned to the hotel room, both were drained, exhausted by the tension of the last few hours. Rath locked the door securely and then sank down on the bed. He had no words and she had too many.

She spoke slowly, her throat dry. 'When I was in

college, I was forced to go to a psychiatrist. They caught me drilling holes in my dorm room floor.'

Rath looked at her, trying to make sense of her words. He could see that she was desperate to explain something to him.

'Why?' he asked. 'Why did you do it?'

Electra shrugged and shook her head. 'I don't know. I was compelled ... I wanted to watch people. The shrink said it went back to my childhood.' She laughed a hollow little chuckle. 'Typical, right? That's what they always say.'

'He couldn't help you?'

Electra shook her head again, more vigorously, more emphatic this time. 'I didn't want him to. Watching people was the only thing I was ever good at. So I started doing it for a living.' She looked at him, as if hoping for something in return.

Her confession had sparked something in him. 'When I was sixteen, I lied about my age and joined the Army,' he said. 'That's where I found out what I was good at...' And they both knew what his special talent was.

There was an awkward moment and Rath looked away. He was not used to opening up and he felt as if he had said too much already. But Electra was ardent, anxious to prevent this moment of intimacy from slipping away.

'Can I ask you something?'

Rath did not answer. She took his silence as assent.

'Am I attractive?'

It was the last thing he expected her to say, but he nodded. 'Yes. Yes, you are.'

'Are you attracted to me?'

'Yes,' he admitted, his voice soft and sincere.

'Is it a physical thing or a mental thing?'

'Both.'

'When did it start?'

'Back in Seattle. In the hotel ... When you were shooting at me.' He sounded shy, like a kid on his first date.

Electra smiled and shook her head slowly. 'You are a strange man, Robert Rath. A very strange man...'

'Joseph,' he said. 'My real name is Joseph.'

From a man like Rath, his real name was a gift more valuable than diamonds, and Electra knew that.

'Joseph...' she said, savoring the word, tasting it. Then she held out her hand. 'I'm Anna. It's awfully nice to meet you.' Her hand was out there like a promise and all Rath had to do was take it. He hesitated a moment, then extended his arm, taking her tiny hand in his huge, hard, callused one. The shock of palm against palm, skin against skin – their first real touch – was galvanizing.

Without another word, they came together, their kisses loving and gentle. Both of them wanted – and desperately needed – contact, the warmth and sympathy of another human being. They fell to the bed ...

The newlyweds in the room next door heard the sounds of passion from the adjacent room; Rath and Electra's lovemaking was prolonged and ardent. The newlyweds giggled and smiled at each other, snuggling down in the bed, knowing exactly what the strangers in the next room were feeling.

A mile away, nestled in the third-floor room of the charred shell of the Hotel Paradiso, Miguel Bain loaded a single round into the chamber of his sniper's rifle and leaned it on the scorched and blistered windowsill. He looked down the scope and sighted it on the apricot he had placed to the side of one of the pillars of the bank.

He could make out the object – a patch of dark in the night that seemed thicker than the surrounding darkness – and he felt his rifle rock steady. He exhaled and squeezed off that single round. A split second later the tiny piece of fruit exploded into a thousand pieces.

Bain smiled as he lowered the rifle. Slowly, solemnly, he raised his index finger to heaven. The next day he would ascend to his rightful place as the best in the business.

And Robert Rath's dream of a new life would be snuffed out.

Chapter Nineteen

The sun blazed the next morning, promising a very hot day. Rath and Electra had risen early, shyly affectionate with each other, more than partners now – but it seemed unreal, as if neither person could quite believe that they had allowed their guards down low enough to fall in love.

Rath logged on with The Contractor, Electra close by his side, reading his questions and the responses.

The Contractor: *The contract has been paid. Transferred to the specified account.*

Rath and Electra looked from the screen to each other. They shared a small smile.

Rath typed: *And the disc?*

The Contractor: *You will be advised. Goodbye, Robert.*

The screen went blank as The Contractor signed out. Rath shut down his own connection to the net and switched off the computer. As Electra poured herself another cup of coffee from the breakfast tray, Rath opened an aluminum-sided case and took out the equipment they would need that day. He had a detailed plan of the Plaza Colon, along with two small hearing aid microphones and transmitters. Electra, an expert in this kind of hardware, scooped up the sets and examined them closely.

'Two-way?' she asked.

Rath nodded. 'That's right.'

Electra frowned at the sets, unhappy at the quality. 'You were scammed,' she announced flatly. 'They saw you coming a mile away. These things are really second-rate. If I had known that we would be using things like these, I would have brought something like—'

She stopped in the middle of her tirade. Rath was staring at her balefully. She smiled and zipped her lips.

'At ten o'clock I'll enter the bank,' he said, referring to the diagram. 'He'll be in the Plaza Colon somewhere. When he sees me go in, he'll move to the hotel.'

'You're sure?' Electra asked. She drained her coffee cup.

Rath nodded. 'Yes, I am.'

'Where will I be?'

He pointed to a spot on the diagram. 'You'll be here at the café. You'll tell me when he goes into the hotel.'

'Then?'

Rath took a deep breath. 'Then we wait.'

Electra poured the last few drops from the coffeepot into her cup. Rath continued with the scheme, not the way he had planned it, but the way he remembered it happening fifteen long years before.

'It'll take all day,' he said, recalling his own tortured day in the Hotel Paradiso. 'He'll begin to doubt himself. He'll start to think he missed me. Then it will start to get dark . . . Time for the bank to close. Say around five-forty, five forty-five ... About that time he'll put down his rifle and he'll go to the bank.'

'But he'll have his pistol with him,' she said.

'The bank has a metal detector,' he said. 'He won't have a gun and neither will I.'

Electra frowned and pursed her lips. 'But what if he doesn't leave the hotel? What then?'

'He will. He will have to. He'll have to see for himself if I'm still in the bank. And when he does, you go into the hotel and take the rifle.'

Electra studied Rath's face for a moment, then held up the earpiece transmitters. 'Let me get this straight ... I tell you when he leaves the hotel. You tell me when he leaves the bank. Is that it?'

Rath nodded. 'That's right.'

'Then what?'

'I'm going to rent a car this morning ... You bring it up and we're gone. Straight to the airport.'

'Simple,' she said.

'In theory.' He slid the .22 out of the holster. 'This is the insurance. Take it. I want you to have it. Just in case.'

Electra looked at the weapon with revulsion and was reluctant to take it. She had lived a strange, subterranean life. Her profession was not without risks – and it was highly illegal – but she had never encountered the possibility of violence. Until Bain had come bursting into her life a few days before she had never seen a gun, never heard one fired for real. The idea of pointing a gun at a human and killing him ... she couldn't even imagine it. At the height of her fear and agitation, back there in the hotel room, she had been unable to kill him. 'I don't think I could shoot someone. I don't think I could even shoot him.'

'Did you ever play Cowboys and Indians when you were a kid?'

'Sure,' said Electra, 'but this – this is different—'

'Which were you? A cowboy or an Indian?'

'An Indian,' said Electra. 'Always an Indian.'

'He's the cowboy,' Rath responded. 'Pull the trigger. You can pretend he'll get up after, when the game is over, but make sure you pull the trigger. He won't hesitate to pull it on you or me. Remember that.'

Electra swallowed hard; this thing was getting a little too real for her. She felt fear creeping up like a prowler.

Rath crossed the Plaza Colon walking quickly. He was dressed in a well-cut suit and tie and he carried an expensive attaché case at his side. He looked like a legitimate, type-A, hurry-up, time-is-money businessman. Of course, there was no such thing as a legitimate businessman on the island, just businessmen of varying degrees of corruption.

When the door of the bank opened, Rath felt the blast of glacial-cold processed air wash over him. In poor countries located in the tropics, prestige was measured in how much air conditioning you could afford. Judging by the wintry atmosphere in this imposing building, the bank was at the top of the heap.

The main trading room was vaulted and vast; the bronze lamp stanchions hanging from the ceiling were elaborate and ornate, burnished bronze that had melted into these rococo fixtures. There were old dark paintings on the wall, and the dim corners were decorated with bronze statuary of a gigantic, overblown grandeur.

The massive clock hanging on the wall above the cage containing the chief cashier showed two minutes after ten...

Electra had taken up her position, sitting at a café table on the edge of the square. She had a perfect view of the side of the hotel and the front of the bank. She placed a thick copy of the latest issue of *Vogue* on the table in front of her along with the *International Herald Tribune* from the day before and a fat paperback novel, the kind of mindless escapist literature that people tended to read on the beach. She looked like that rarest of travelers to the island, a pretty tourist who had taken a day off from the surf and sun to do a little sight-seeing in the old town and had chosen to take a break at the café. She ordered a cup of coffee and the waiter brought her a cup of espresso so strong it had the consistency of syrup and packed enough caffeine to keep a less experienced coffee drinker awake for a week.

She slipped on her sunglasses and looked around the Plaza Colon. As she looked, Rath's voice crackled in her ear.

'I'm in the bank,' he said. His voice was hardly higher than a whisper and he sounded as if he were miles away, not just a matter of a few hundred yards. Silently, Electra cursed the cheapness and unreliability of the equipment. Why hadn't Rath consulted a *professional* ... like her.

'Where is he?' Rath asked.

Electra scanned the plaza, nervous, edgy. 'I don't see him,' she said, the tension clear in her voice. 'I—'

There he was on the far side of the square. Bain was

gliding through the crowded space like a shark in a school of minnows. He was making for the Hotel Paradiso.

'He's here,' Electra whispered. 'He's here.'

A waiter set down a second cup of espresso in front of her. She seized the little cup and, in her nervousness, drank down the hot, muddy, nerve-jolting liquid in a single gulp. She watched as Bain disappeared between a gap in the boarded-up door of the burned-out hotel. He was gone in an instant, vanishing as if he had never been there.

'He's going in,' she said. 'He's in the hotel.'

Rath heard the fright in her voice and smiled to himself. 'That's what we want. Relax. Try having a cup of decaf.'

'Very funny . . .'

Rath broke off the transmission abruptly, fished a piece of paper from his inside coat pocket and stepped up to the teller's cage.

'May I help you, sir?' The teller smiled unctuously. All of the customers of the bank were very rich. The teller had learned long ago that they would tolerate nothing less than absolute subservience. It always paid off.

Rath slid the withdrawal slip across the smooth marble counter. 'Yes. Could you check on a transfer for me?'

'Of course, sir.'

'If everything is in order,' said Rath evenly, 'I would like to make a cash withdrawal. Today.'

'Very good, sir.' Then the man looked down and saw the size of the figure. The oleaginous politeness vanished. He swallowed hard. 'One moment, please.'

The man scurried away to speak to an officer of the bank. A transaction of this size was well beyond his authority.

Chapter Twenty

———◆———

Bain had made his way to room 302 in the shell of the burned-out hotel. He reached overhead, thrusting his hand into some charred, half-collapsed timbers, and pulled down the silenced sniper's rifle. As he checked the weapon, he stepped to the window and surveyed the square below. The market was in full swing, thronged with shoppers; a few people were drinking their morning coffee at the café to the left – and dead ahead of him was the bank. Bringing the weapon to his shoulder, he looked along the barrel into the burning glare of the morning sun, aiming for the front door of the bank. A man was leaving the bank and Bain placed the crosshairs of the scope on the man's forehead. Bain pulled the trigger and the mechanism clicked. Had there been a round in the chamber, the man would now have been sprawled on the ground, his brains splattered on the facade of the bank, the dark cranial blood pumping onto the warm cobblestones.

But the man continued blithely on his way, unaware of how close he had come to sudden death.

Bain was pleased with the little performance. He slapped a magazine into the rifle and placed the weapon against the wall. He took up his position by the window, his eyes fixed on the front door of the bank. In his bag he had the provisions he would need that day: some fruit, some bottled water and his entertainment. First, Bain peeled a luscious blood orange and sucked a segment into his mouth, relishing the sweet juice and the soft pulp. Then from the bag he pulled out a small keyboard and a set of headphones. Plugging in the phones, he put his fingers on the keyboard and began to play. The music was of his own composition and it soothed him. He played well, improvising endless variations on a series of musical themes, his hands moving gracefully; his gaze at the bank never wavering.

The teller disappeared into the rear offices of the bank and emerged a moment later leading a portly, well-dressed man. He carried a printed receipt and he wore a great big smile on his face.

'Señor,' he said deferentially. 'We have received your transfer.'

He handed the receipt to Rath, who checked the numbers – a two followed by seven zeros. All in order.

'I want to close this account,' said Rath smoothly. 'Could you get the paperwork together as soon as possible?'

The banker's genial smile faded. 'As soon as possible? Do you mean today?' he said, alarmed at the very idea.

'That's what I mean,' said Rath.

It was as if the man were not quite sure what he had heard. 'You wish to close the account *today*?'

Rath nodded solemnly. He had no wish to make a joke. This was deadly serious business to him. 'If you please.'

'Yes. Very good.' No bank, no matter how rich, wants to give up a huge sum of money on the spur of the moment, but this bank had a reputation for a certain ... flexibility. That sort of notoriety was worth millions in more shady money. If they failed to honor this request, word might get around and business would flow to the competition.

'And how would you like the money?' the official asked after a quick internal struggle.

'American currency.'

The man nodded like a waiter approving of a customer's choice of appetizer. 'Very good, sir... If you could just wait a moment...' He gestured and caught the eye of a man on the far side of the bank, the one man in the building even more formally dressed. It was the president of the bank himself.

He stepped over immediately and conferred with his underling for a moment, the two men speaking Spanish rapidly. Occasionally the president glanced at Rath, but mostly he listened. Finally the great man himself spoke.

'We will be glad to honor your request, sir,' said the bank president. 'But you must be aware that there is a ... a withdrawal fee. For a sum of this size I have to warn you, it could be quite a significant amount.'

'I am fully aware of that.'

The president nodded at his subordinate who bowed to his boss and to Rath, then hurried away to do as he was told. The bank president looked back at Rath. 'You understand that this will take some time.'

'I have all day,' said Rath with a smile.

'If you would care to come back in a few hours...'

'I'll wait here if you don't mind.'

The bank was about to make four million for a single day's work. The bank president did not mind in the least. 'The bank and the staff are at your disposal, sir,' he said. 'If you require anything, do not hesitate to ask.'

By early afternoon the sun was high in the sky, a white globe beating down relentlessly on the island. Activity in the square had just about ceased, the market workers having faded away to pass the siesta hours in the cool shade. By contrast, the café was busy as the more affluent went there to eat their lunch and to drink iced drinks and pass the afternoon in the shade. Electra dined as well and tried to relax, but despite the fact that the food was excellent, she had little interest in it. Her stomach was still churning from a combination of too much strong coffee and the tension of the situation.

Rath lunched luxuriously, the bank president insisting that he avail himself of the services of the private chef kept on staff for the most senior employees. He had a three-course lunch at a table set with crisp linens and heavy silver, dining alone, reading an airmail edition of *The Financial Times*. The bank president sent over a bottle of Chateau Margaux '75, which Rath declined with regrets.

Miguel Bain could not recall having been so miserable – even getting caught in a gas explosion had been preferable to this: at least that had been over in less than a second. He had been in his roost for only three hours and already it felt as if a hundred years had passed since he had strolled so cockily across the plaza earlier that morning.

He sat in the charred chair, his clothing sodden with sweat. The room was as hot as a forge fire, the merciless heat baking it, raising the temperature so high it was difficult to breathe. His gaze was still fixed on the bank; stinging sweat was dripping from his forehead, yet he was afraid to blink for fear of missing his mark. He dug out a handkerchief and rubbed his eyes – but he did one eye at a time; the other remained on the huge doors of the bank. To check his watch he raised his wrist to eye level rather than risk looking down. Time passed so slowly.

'What are you doing in there?' he moaned. 'Come on, Rath. You cannot stay in there for ever. You'll have to come out eventually. Why waste the time?'

Then – *there*! A man dressed like Rath was coming out of the bank. For a moment, Bain could not move, afraid that the figure was nothing more than a mirage. Then he sprung into action, his body snapping erect. He seized the rifle in his sweat-slick hands and aimed, lining up the sights. Then the adrenaline rush fizzled. It wasn't Rath – it didn't even look like him. Bain's mind was playing tricks on him.

Suddenly he slapped himself violently across the face, enjoying, even appreciating the pain and the clarity it brought. Bain wiped the sweat from his forehead, leaving a smear of black powder in its place. Fumbling for his bag, he pulled out a container of bottled water and drank thirstily, never once taking his eyes off the bank.

'Relax, baby,' he said to himself. '*Calmate . . .*'

As the sun traced its arc through the sky, the shadows in the plaza lengthened, stretching toward the bank. After lunch Rath returned to the main floor of the bank and settled in a cool, high-backed leather chair, watching the traffic in the room. The big clock read 3:10 . . .

'Talk to me,' he said, his voice low.

At her table Electra glanced at the hotel. Her lunch dishes had been cleared and there was yet another coffee cup in front of her.

'There's no sign of him,' she whispered. 'He's just sitting up there, same as us.'

'No, no,' said Rath, 'I don't mean that.'

'What *do* you mean?'

'I mean talk to me. Tell me some of that weird stuff you know.'

Electra smiled and thought for a moment. An old man wandered by, a beat-up, sweat-stained fedora on his head. The ragged hat gave her an idea.

'You know the expression "as mad as a hatter"?'

'That's from *Alice in Wonderland*, isn't it?'

'Yes, but it's a real thing. Hatmakers, hatters, they used mercurous nitrate to make felt hats. The trouble was, they would absorb it through their skin and some of them went insane. No one knew why at the time. Nobody cared as long as their hats fit.'

Rath was amused by this little fact. 'Tell me another one.'

There was silence for a moment, then Electra spoke. 'Well, while we're on the subject of insanity, you know "Mad as a March hare"?'

'What's that, rabbit hatmakers?'

Electra laughed. 'No, not quite . . . Hares are bold, wild in March. March is when they mate . . . I believe the correct term is rutting. Wild rutting bull bunnies . . .'

Miguel Bain gritted his teeth and rocked from side to

side. He had to take a piss and he had to do it bad. A few men came out of the bank, and he tried to distract himself by examining each one of them, hoping that one would be Rath, but his full bladder continued to divert his attention.

'*Esta es una locura,*' he hissed. He snatched up his empty water bottle, unzipped his pants and began refilling it.

By contrast, Rath relieved himself in the cool, elegant bathroom of the bank, washing his hands at the basin and drying them with a blindingly white towel. He looked at himself in the wide mirror as the bathroom attendant brushed off his suit. There was not a trace of sweat on his brow.

It was very difficult to urinate in a bottle without looking. Bain had already wandered off course a couple of times, splashing urine on his pants and on the floor, but he still kept the bank in sight. All of a sudden, a man emerged from the bank. Rath!

Bain dropped the warm bottle, splashing himself with more urine, and without bothering to zip up, he fell on his rifle, raised it and came within a micron of squeezing off a shot. But once again the figure was not Rath. Bain's curses were so loud and so intense that they seemed to raise the temperature in the burned-out room.

Not even a world-class caffeine addict like Electra could stomach another dose of the coffee served in the café. The waiter was approaching with her ninth refill but she waved him off.

'*No más,*' she said. '*No más.*'

The hands of the big clock clicked from 5:10 to 5:11 and Rath could see that the workday was coming to an end. Like office employees everywhere, as the day drew in, the workers in the bank eased up. Phones weren't answered on the first ring; typing was carried on with a little less brio than earlier in the day. All over the cavernous room came the sound of file drawers sliding shut and computers shutting down.

The bank president himself approached Rath. 'Señor,' he said, 'we have deducted our fee and we are making a second count in the cash room. The funds should be available in one half hour.'

'Thank you,' said Rath.

'I thank you, sir,' said the bank president, 'for your business and for your patience.'

Rath thought to himself that hanging around a bank for seven hours was a pretty soft way of making sixteen million dollars. Soft, that is, if he could get out of there alive . . .

Bain was just a knot of nerves in the window of room 302. The sun was low now, filling the room with golden light, and he had to squint against the still powerful rays to make sure that he was seeing all the movement at the front door of the bank. And the action was heating up. As the workday ended, people started leaving in groups – three or four secretaries at a time, a gaggle of tellers, two middle managers walking out together to have a drink and a gossip session before going home. Every time the big doors swung open, Bain had to scan every face through the scope to make sure that Rath was not making his escape in a knot of bank employees. The workers laughed and talked, relieved that the work day had come to an end and that they could turn their attention to more pleasant things. Not one of them had the slightest idea that they were under a gun, that a single mistake or moment of lack of control on Bain's part and they would be dead.

But Rath was nowhere to be seen. Anger took hold of Bain and he slammed the stock of the rifle into the floor, splintering a floorboard already weakened by the fire. He checked his watch. It was 5:47. In fewer than fifteen minutes the bank would close. Doubts plagued him. Maybe Rath had managed to escape in a momentary lapse of vigilance; maybe there was another way out of the bank and Rath had left hours ago ... Maybe he was already off the island, sipping champagne in the first class cabin of an airliner, patting the big fat case full of money – money that belonged to Miguel Bain.

Suddenly, Bain stood up, the stiff joints in his knees and ankles cracking painfully. He had to know what was going on...

Electra glanced idly at the hotel, expecting to see nothing she hadn't seen all day – nothing at all – then sat bolt upright, shocked. Bain was there, climbing through the broken doorway and making his way across the square.

'He's coming,' Electra almost shouted and then forced herself to whisper. 'He's coming. He's left the hotel and he's heading for the bank.'

Rath glanced at the clock and frowned. 'He waited four minutes longer than I did,' he said. He had to give Bain a certain amount of credit for sticking it out – four minutes was an eternity under those conditions.

But there was no way Electra could have known that. 'What? What did you say?'

'Never mind,' said Rath urgently. 'Go.'

Electra tossed a handful of bills on the table and walked away from the café, the waiter swooping down like a hawk to examine his extravagant tip. A moment later she reached the door of the hotel, peering into the musty gloom, feeling a fear more intense than any she had ever known before. She had to force herself to enter, placing her feet carefully, picking her way through the rubble, making for the rickety staircase.

The bank president approached Rath from the far side of the huge room. A uniformed security guard trailed behind him. In his left hand was Rath's briefcase and he could tell by the way the man walked that it was very heavy.

'Where are you?' Rath whispered into the microphone.

Electra had made it to the third floor. 'I'm about to enter three-o-two,' she said. She pushed open the door and caught the gamy smell of sun-baked sweat and urine in the room. The acrid stench hit the back of her throat and she coughed, but she managed to speak. 'I'm in,' she gasped.

'Good. Get the rifle and get out of there.'

The only problem was, the weapon was nowhere to be found. She scanned the floor, checked behind a blackened mattress – nothing. She noted the orange peels and the empty water bottles littering the floor and told herself that she was in the right room – but the rifle wasn't.

'It's not here,' she gasped into the transmitter. 'The rifle is not here.'

Rath felt his stomach lurch. 'Get out of there,' he ordered. 'Forget the rifle.'

Electra looked through a hole in the lathing, peering into the room next door. The rifle wasn't there either.

'I told you to get out of there!'

As she turned to go, though, she spotted the slender weapon stashed up in the rafters above her head. 'Wait!' she yelped. 'I got it.' She grabbed the rifle and held it close, as if it were a baby that might slip from her grasp. It was surprisingly heavy, but she didn't care. The gun was warm from the heat of the room and still slick from the sweat and oils on Bain's hand. It was an ungainly burden, the long barrel and extended silencer made the weapon difficult to manage in the cramped confines of the room. Where Rath and Bain handled a gun like that as if it was tailor made for them, to Electra it was a foreign body, an awkward encumbrance. But at that very moment, all she wanted was to get out of there as fast as possible.

Relief replaced nausea in Rath's stomach. 'Okay,' he commanded. 'Go. Now. Get out of there.'

Bain was at the door of the bank now. Rath pulled the transmitter from his ear and pocketed it. If Bain had spotted it – and Rath knew he would have – he would have known in an instant what was going on. There was a manic, almost insane gleam in the young man's eyes and he seemed to burn with anger . . .

In the normal course of events, Electra hated being given orders, particularly by a man. But this one she was very pleased to be able to carry out. She raced for the door, not caring where her feet fell. She stepped hard on a charred planking and suddenly the floor seemed to open up and swallow her. She fell straight down until the sharp boards dug into her flesh, wedging her rib-deep in the hole. She screamed out in pain and fright. But no one heard her cries . . .

Chapter Twenty-One

———◆———

Soaked with sweat, his face streaked with grime and soot, Bain pushed open the heavy glass doors of the bank and strode inside. Just across the threshold he stopped and looked around. Then he saw Rath sitting in his comfortable chair, the very picture of cool, a man seemingly without a care in the world. Bain was confused by the exhausting events of the day, and oddly enough his first reaction was to run away. Rath looked calm and cold-blooded at the same time, a man plainly in charge of his fate. A man unlikely to allow himself to be killed by a bedraggled, addled man like this.

But Miguel Bain forced himself to take a deep breath and walk to where Rath sat. It was all he could do to walk normally. His legs felt rubbery under him and his gait was unsteady, like a drunk. Bain was breathing hard and the sound seemed to fill his ears. The security guard was looking at him curiously, wondering if he should intervene. But Bain paid him no mind. He fixed his eyes on Rath and walked toward him like a man lost in the desert stumbling toward an oasis – and praying it wasn't a mirage.

'How did you know?' he demanded, his voice hoarse and fractured. 'Who told you I would be coming for you?'

'Nicolai,' said Rath.

'Nicolai?' For a moment, Bain looked bewildered, as if he couldn't place the name. 'Nicolai? Nicolai the *Russian*?'

Rath nodded. 'That's right.'

'But he's dead.' Bain's eyes darted around the room, nervously looking at anyone who might venture near to them. The bank president and the security guard stood a few yards away, waiting for Rath 'to finish his conversation before drawing near. Both men looked with suspicion on the bedraggled Bain. The banker wondered if he should send the security guard over to see the fellow out, but he thought the better of it. Rath appeared to know him.

'Fifteen years ago I walked into this bank,' Rath explained. 'I looked just like you. I was in a similar state of mind too.' Rath looked at Bain with something like pity on his face. 'And I know what you're thinking right now . . .'

'Do you?' said Bain sarcastically.

Rath nodded. 'You think you've been sold out. You don't trust anyone. It's the first and last commandment of our profession. It's what keeps you alive. So no matter what I say, you won't believe me, will you? Ironic, isn't it?'

Bain's face was twisted with anger. 'And who can you trust, Rath? No one. You're alone. Same as me.'

Rath shook his head slowly. If only Bain knew how

wrong he was ... To a man like Bain, the idea of trusting another human being was anathema. It was like a piece of a puzzle that couldn't be made to fit into the framework of an assassin's life. Bain thought that Rath had finally given up.

It was almost closing time and the last employees were moving toward the exit. Soon the two men would be alone in the vast hall except for a few bank officers and the guards.

'This is where the rules change,' said Rath evenly. 'That man over there is holding a briefcase containing eight million dollars that belongs to me.' Chivalrously, Rath did not think that Electra should pay to buy off Bain. In Rath's world the man always picked up the check. 'I'll give you half, four million, if you'll just walk away.'

Suddenly, Bain didn't look so nervous. He grinned mischievously. 'I've heard this offer before,' he said. 'But from a mark, Rath, not from an assassin.' He laughed brightly. 'I tell you now, that night in the cab – I thought I was lucky to come out of that. But now I think different. *Te pusiste dischoso.*'

To be honest, Rath had not expected Bain to have the sense to accept his offer, but it was worth a try. 'I could offer you a hundred million dollars and you would still say the same stupid thing, wouldn't you? I'm willing to pay you four million dollars to save your own life. And it's not enough, is it?'

Bain shook his head. 'That's right. I'm going to take you. Today.' Rath should have expected the reaction. Just as he had no interest in money – except as insurance against the vicissitudes of life – so it was with Bain. This was about being the best, about fearing no man on earth.

'You're wrong,' said Rath. 'Today, I take you.'

Bain turned on his heel. 'No more chit-chat,' he said over his shoulder. He strode angrily for the exit.

The instant he left the bank, Rath reinserted the earpiece. 'Electra, where are you?' The only answer was the babbling of harsh static. Rath frowned. 'Electra, can you hear me?'

The only thing Electra could hear was the panicky sound of her own shallow breathing. She jammed her hands on the floorboards and pushed, desperately trying to pull herself free. Panic was beginning to set in and she wasted a lot of strength and effort struggling in vain to extricate herself. The splintered boards were jabbing into her like fish hooks, pinning her to the spot.

Doing her best to beat back her debilitating hysteria, Electra tried to take control of herself. She breathed in deep and then slowly, painfully, carefully, she tried to ease herself out of the trap. She bit her lip to fight off the pain and she strained every muscle attempting to extricate herself. Almost out, her muscles gave way and she surrendered to the effort and the agony.

But she knew she couldn't give up now. 'Next time,' she gasped. 'I'll get out next time. Definitely.'

The bank president and the guard stepped over to Rath. They were anxious to be rid of him – it had been a long day for them as well.

'Everything is in order, señor,' the official said, gesturing toward the briefcase. He snapped his fingers at the guard, who opened the attaché case, displaying the wads of money within. The bills were high denomination, but grimy and frayed. They had been in circulation so long they had become absolutely anonymous, impossible to trace.

Rath nodded. 'I won't bother to count it.'

'You are welcome to do so, señor.' He had to make the offer, but he was praying that Rath did not avail himself of the chance to do so. It would take one man many, many hours to count the contents of the attaché case. But Rath let him off the hook.

'There is no need,' said Rath.

The bank president cleared his throat and looked a little embarrassed. He did not meet Rath's eyes as he spoke. 'This is awkward,' he said. 'Not really my affair, you understand ... But I was told you would be giving us something in return for the money.'

'I understand,' said Rath. The Contractor had planned this down to the last detail. As he handed over the disc, the bank president pulled a handheld disc scanner from his pocket. He slid the piece of plastic into the slot and waited a moment while the device read the information. A green light clicked on, indicating that this was the real disc, the one The Contractor wanted so desperately. For an instant, Rath wondered what was really on that disc – what had been worth all those killings. But then he realized he didn't care – it didn't mean anything to him now. He was leaving that secretive and surreptitious life behind for ever. There would be no tears for his old life; it was as dead now as one of his marks.

The banker looked relieved and said something in Spanish to the guard. The man passed the briefcase to Rath.

'And now,' the bank president said, a little smile on his face, 'we are closed, señor.' The man seemed very relieved.

The big clock on the wall read 6:03 p.m.

Electra was still struggling like an animal caught in a trap, trying to claw her way out of the hole, gaining a few inches of freedom with every attempt. She was completely drenched with perspiration and every muscle in her body was aching, but she knew she couldn't give up.

Rocking and wiggling in the opening, she was freeing herself an inch at a time, working herself free as if she were a cork jammed into the neck of a bottle. She stopped to rest for a moment, panting from the exertion. In that moment of silence she heard a sound that made her nauseated with fear. Three floors below, Bain came crashing through the door of the hotel and started for the stairs.

'Oh my God,' she whispered. She summoned up all her strength and forced herself out of the thicket of splintered wood and plaster; ignoring the pain, she grappled and fought, pulling herself free. As she tugged her legs out, she flopped down on the scorched floor, panting, spent from the exertion and immobilized by the fear. But she knew she couldn't stop now...

When Bain burst into the room, Electra was nowhere to be seen. It had not occurred to Bain that Rath might have had an accomplice in the hotel – assassins worked alone – so he did not even bother to look for signs of a confederate. He did not even notice that the rifle had been moved.

Snatching the gun, he dove for the window and aimed carefully. 'Come on, *orgulloso toro*,' he whispered, willing Rath out of the bank. 'I have the sword right here. There's no shame. I promise you won't feel a thing...'

A moment later, Bain got his wish. The big door swung

open and Rath stepped into the twilight of the Plaza Colon. It was not quite a clean shot and Bain knew that he had to wait for the perfect moment. He knew he would only have one shot. If he missed, he lost. 'Take a step,' Bain murmured quietly. 'Just one little step.'

Bain could see him so clearly. Rath peered from side to side, looking for something. He seemed puzzled. His lips moved, as if he were speaking to someone, but the plaza was almost deserted; there was not a soul within earshot.

'What are you doing, Rath? What game are you playing?' He adjusted the crosshairs of the sniper's scope, the X settling on Rath's forehead. 'Look up,' Bain urged. 'I want to see your eyes.'

Electra was hiding behind the mattress leaning against the wall. She held the pistol so tight her knuckles were turning white. She knew what she had to do, but she couldn't. Bain was not a cowboy and she was not an Indian.

Slowly, Rath looked up, and saw the long silencer of the rifle jutting from the window, the shadow of the shooter behind it. He was seconds away from being a dead man, but the worst part was not knowing where Electra was. Had she deserted? Was she in trouble? Was she still alive? But he knew in another second, it wouldn't matter.

Bain was about to pull the trigger when he noticed the microphone in Rath's ear, the cord snaking under his shirt to the transmitter taped to his chest. Bain started with shock. Rath was talking to someone – he was working with someone. Bain lowered the rifle and sniffed the air. Behind the rank smell of the ruined building, the stench of his own sweat and urine, he could make out a familiar smell.

'Jasmine...' he whispered. Bain turned suddenly and looked straight into the barrel of Electra's .22.

Electra shrugged, as if apologising. 'Howdy,' she said. 'Sorry about this.' She yanked the trigger and Bain's shoulder turned dark red.

Chapter Twenty-Two

———◆◆◆———

Bain dropped the rifle, grabbed his bag and dove to his right, crashing through the wall. Electra fired at him but missed. Bain stumbled into the room next door, missed his footing and fell heavily, the boards opening up like thin ice. He tumbled to the second floor.

Electra forced herself to step up to the edge of the ragged hole and peer down. Bain's bag lay there, but there was no sign of the man. Suddenly, bullet holes started opening up at her feet as Bain, beneath her, fired up at the sound of her footsteps. There was no warning blast, just bullets silently drilling the floor at her feet. Electra yelped and ran, scared to death that the boards would give way under her. She had to get down and out of that death trap of a building.

Electra bolted for the stairs and dashed to the first landing. Bain was waiting for her. She froze mid-step and looked at him, her eyes wide with fear. Bain wasn't going to make a speech or a sarcastic remark. He was

173

going to kill her. The gun came up. Electra could see straight down the barrel.

'Bain!'

He swung around, caught the merest glimpse of Rath, but in an instant he was gone. When Bain turned back to the stairs, Electra had vanished as well.

'Two against one, Rath,' Bain yelled. 'Is that your edge? You didn't take the mark, man. You took the bribe.' His voice was filled with contempt. Bain started up the stairs. 'I'll take her first, Rath, I'll even up the odds.'

From somewhere in the building, Electra shouted, 'I think he's serious, Rath.'

'Bet on it,' Bain screamed.

Rath pulled himself through a hole in the floor, breaking into room 205. 'You've got something of mine, Electra.'

That could only mean the gun. She looked at the .22 in her hand and guessed where Rath might be.

'When do you want it back?'

'Now!'

Rath appeared in the room below Electra and she tossed the gun to him, his hand closing around the handle of the weapon as Bain fired. A split second later Rath felt the searing hot pain as a bullet creased his shoulder. He fell and rolled, returning fire.

Light played through the broken lathing in the walls, the tortured timbers of the building creaking and groaning. Rath, Electra and Bain crept through the ruined hotel in a heart-stopping game of cat and mouse in a collapsing maze.

The full length of the third floor hallway stretched out

ahead. Electra stepped out from a room and saw Rath at the far end.

'Thank God,' she whispered as she started down the corridor.

Suddenly, Bain appeared at a door behind her. Electra didn't know it but she was about to be caught in a hellacious crossfire.

Rath dashed forward. 'Down!' As Electra hit the deck, Bain jumped forward with a wild scream. The two men unloaded their weapons, silenced bullets howling and whining in the enclosed space.

Rath's feet pounded on the rotten boards and suddenly his right leg drilled through, yanking him to a sinew-straining stop. As he sunk, he fired, a slug slamming into the meat of Bain's thigh. The force of impact picked Bain up and threw him back. As he hit the floor, the boards cracked and opened and he fell to the next landing. He crashed through that and tumbled farther, dropping all the way to the ground floor. Bain landed in a heap of rubble – charred beam, broken glass, jagged chunks of concrete – and did not move.

Three floors above, Rath reached for Electra's hand. 'Okay,' he said, guiding her. 'Let's get the hell out of here.'

'Thank God...'

'Where were you?' Rath asked. 'What were you playing at? What happened?' He was joyful and furious at the same time – pleased that she had come through this, but angry that she had put him through such torture.

'I got stuck.'

'Stuck! Do you have any idea how worried I was? How

crazy you made me?' He was like a hectoring parent scolding a child for coming in after curfew.

'Sorry,' Electra said sheepishly. She let him rage on, knowing that he was just blowing off steam, decompressing after the intensity of the day.

Rath led her to the stairs and they walked slowly down to the lobby. Before they left the hotel, they stopped and looked at Bain's body half-buried in debris. Rath was not finished venting his pent-up tension.

'Sorry? Goddammit! I told you—'

'That's no way to speak to a lady.' The voice was male and it came from the shadows. A chill coursed down Rath's spine. He turned and saw a man step out of the gloom behind Electra. He was holding a gun to her head.

'Hello, Robert . . . It's been a long time.' The man spoke with a slight accent.

'Nicolai,' said Rath, stunned. In an instant his mind raced all the way to that hot day fifteen years before – the day he killed the man standing in front of him.

'Or, if you prefer,' he said, 'you can call me The Contractor.'

Chapter Twenty-Three

———•◆•———

'Drop the gun, please,' said Nicolai. He edged a few inches closer to Electra, the gun steady in his hand. There was no way Rath could have taken out Nicolai before he blew her away. He had no choice but to drop the gun.

'You must be the mark,' said Nicolai, throwing a sidelong glance at Electra. 'You are a thief. You caused me trouble.'

With his free hand, Nicolai pulled the disc from his pocket. 'I had to use both of my best to track you down,' he told her. He looked over at Bain. 'Is that Bain?'

Rath nodded. 'That's him.'

'I never imagined that he was so young,' said Nicolai. 'It's a shame he had to die. But I think it was meant to be. He was second best after all.'

With his free hand, Nicolai picked up the attaché case. The moment of truth was at hand. But there was something Rath had to get straight before the end came.

'You're my Contractor,' he said. 'All these years and it was you on the other end of the line.'

Nicolai nodded. 'Life's a strange circle, Rath. Things end at beginnings and begin at endings.' He shrugged. 'I don't pretend to understand it myself.'

Rath's mind swirled with a dozen questions and he managed to squeeze one through gritted teeth. It was the most basic question of all. 'Why?'

Nicolai nodded; he would give Rath his explanation. He deserved that much. 'I saw the Cold War ending. *I needed to die.* I could not leave a past behind to contaminate the new life ahead. It's as simple as that.'

'I killed you,' said Rath. 'I saw it. I saw you fall.'

Nicolai opened his jacket to reveal a bulletproof vest. 'You always went for the heart, Robert. That made you predictable. And you know that's a sin in our profession.'

Nicolai swung the gun in a wide arc, pointing it at Rath. Electra thought she was going to burst from the tension, but Rath just stared down the barrel and into Nicolai's dark eyes. All those years, he thought, all those years of remorse, of pain and heart-ache over the death of Nicolai... And he had been nothing more than a cog in a machine, part of a plan to make Nicolai a rich and powerful man. The weight of the betrayal hit him like a hammer.

'You son of a bitch...'

'No,' said Nicolai with a little shake of his head. 'Not really. You delivered me. Now I am going to deliver you.'

As Nicolai aimed, Rath felt the faintest tug on the cuff of his pants. It took all the self-control in the world to stop him looking down, but he knew what was going on. Bain was alive.

'Good-bye, old friend,' said Nicolai. There seemed to be genuine regret in his voice.

But before he could pull the trigger, Rath dove to his right, opening a clear space for Bain.

'*Colgo los tenis!*' he screamed as his .22 came up and a single shot drilled Nicolai, slamming into his eye and lodging deep in his brain. His heart stopped mid-beat and he toppled like a felled statue.

Rath came up from the floor, his own gun in his hand. Bain and Rath had each other covered. But neither man fired. Neither man wanted to.

'I can't watch this,' Electra muttered.

There was a long moment of silence, then Bain thrust out his hand. '*Ayudame...*' he said. 'Help me up, will you?'

Rath took his hand and pulled Bain from the rubble. The young man was bloody, bruised and covered in filth. He smelled terrible. But he was alive. His eyes fell on Nicolai.

'King's castle to black queen six,' he said.

Rath shook his head. 'No more. I'm leaving the game behind. You younger players can have it now.'

The look on Bain's face turned thoughtful as he considered the implications of this statement. 'That would make me number one,' he said.

'I can live with that. Can you?'

Bain grinned. '*Absolutamente. Compañeros.*' He pulled the gun away, aiming it toward the ceiling. He pulled the trigger and the firing mechanism merely clicked. 'I was out of bullets anyway,' he said, his face split by a big grin.

179

Rath didn't care. Finally he had the chance to do what he had been aching to do – that is, take Electra in his arms. But he had taken only two steps toward her when Bain drew a second weapon and lowered it, pointing it squarely at the back of Rath's head. The grin was gone now and his voice was cold and steely.

Rath froze when he heard the weapon cock.

'As long as you're out there, even retired, I'll never be number one. Never the best. Rath, you become the champ by knocking out the champ. You know that...'

If nothing else, Rath was going to die feeling like a damn fool – he knew that there was nothing he could say, no way he could convince Bain to let him off the hook. He was dealing with a man's pride here and that was an obstacle he could not overcome.

'You two want to say good-bye?' Bain asked.

Rath really had nothing more to say. His were the saddest eyes Electra had ever seen. As if to cut off his gaze, Electra put on her sunglasses, a thick, dark carapace locking him out, as she apparently withdrew from the contest.

Rath looked at her ruefully. But he couldn't bring himself to blame her for anything. This was self-preservation after all. With Nicolai dead, she was no longer a mark. Maybe she wouldn't escape with the money, but she would live...

Then he noticed something, his eyes flickering wide as he saw Bain reflected in the dark lenses of her sunglasses. Rath knew exactly where Bain was – and Electra knew exactly what she was doing. As Bain's finger tightened on the trigger, the side of Rath's jacket blew open a gaping hole as he shot backwards straight through the cloth, like a Wild West trick shooter.

The single bullet smashed into Bain's heart and he fell, going down hard. His eyes were dull with death, but they flickered for a moment in admiration. 'Bravo,' he gasped. 'Bravo...'

Those were his last words.

Maybe it was Hawaii, perhaps it was some speck of island land in Micronesia – Rath and Electra would never tell. There they used the money to build themselves a little house by the lagoon, where they passed their days quietly. They made love often. Pearl watched jealously.

Electra had a lot of time to read. Occasionally she would look up from her book and say something like: 'Do you know why dogs have black lips?'

And Rath would sigh and smile and say, 'No, but I have a bad feeling you're going to tell me...'

The Advocate's Devil

A stunning courtroom drama in the tradition of PRESUMED INNOCENT

Alan M. Dershowitz

What do you do if you're a defence attorney – and you suspect your client is guilty? When Abe Ringel takes on the defence of a professional basketball player accused of rape, he thinks he's found a 'can't lose' case. Joe Campbell is handsome and charismatic; his alleged victim went voluntarily to his hotel room; countless 'groupies' would give their eyeteeth to sleep with him. But is he as perfect as he seems?

As the case progresses, evidence mounts up to suggest that Campbell may be guilty. Caught between his professional ethics and his heart, Abe faces the most painful dilemma of his life. How can he provide a winning defence – when he knows his client may be a threat to women?

FICTION / THRILLER 0 7472 5103 7

Martina Cole

DANGEROUS LADY

SHE'S GOT LONDON'S BIGGEST VILLAINS IN THE PALM OF
HER HAND . . .

Ducking and diving is a way of life down Lancaster Road: all
the Ryans are at it. But Michael, the eldest, has ambitions way
beyond petty crime. His little sister, Maura, turns a blind eye to
her beloved brother's misdeeds – until they cost her the only
man she's ever cared about. And then Maura decides to forget
love and romance and join the family 'firm'.

No one thinks a seventeen-year-old blonde can take on the
hard men of London's gangland, but it's a mistake to
underestimate Maura Ryan: she's tough, clever and beautiful –
and she's determined not to be hurt again. Which makes her
one very dangerous lady.

Together, she and Michael are unbeatable: the Queen and
King of organised crime, they run the pubs and clubs, the
prostitutes and pimps of the West End. With Maura
masterminding it, they pull off an audacious gold bullion
robbery and have much of the Establishment in their pockets.

But notoriety has its price. The police are determined to put
away Maura once and for all – and not everyone in the family
thinks that's such a bad idea. When it comes to the crunch,
Maura has to face the pain of lost love in her past – and the
dangerous lady discovers her heart is not made entirely of
stone.

'A £150,000 success story . . . her tale of gang warfare and
romance centred on an Irish immigrant family in 1950s
London' *Daily Mail*

FICTION / GENERAL 0 7472 3932 0

MILK AND HONEY

A PETER DECKER WHODUNNIT

FAYE KELLERMAN

'Faye Kellerman establishes herself as a unique voice in crime fiction. The central character of Peter Decker is unforgettable' James Ellroy, author of *The Black Dahlia*

Sergeant Peter Decker is driving through a modern housing estate late one night when he discovers an abandoned toddler wearing blood-stained pyjamas. No one claims the curly-headed girl and Decker and his partner, Marge Dunn, resolve to find her parents as soon as possible.

Noticing bee-stings all over the child's arm, they go on a hunt that takes them to a honey farm set in the barren scrubland surrounding Los Angeles. It's a tough landscape, the people work hard and have little time for city folk, so the two detectives aren't surprised when no welcoming party is there to receive them. Nothing, though, has prepared them for the incredible stonewalling from the locals, nor for the grisly sight that greets them in the farmhouse. But Decker and Dunn are professionals to the core and, delving deeper, find themselves stirring up a gruesome mystery far more lethal than the ordinary hornets' nest . . .

Some reviews for Faye Kellerman:

'A tour de force that shouldn't be missed . . . a stellar performance' *Publishers Weekly*

'Excellent story of rape and murder' *Time Out*

'Irresistibly plotted' *Financial Times*

FICTION / CRIME 0 7472 3430 2

JOHN FRANCOME

BREAK NECK

'Francome writes an odds-on racing cert'
Daily Express

When apprentice jockey Rory Gillespie
abandons his fiancée Laura Brickhill, in favour
of trainer's daughter Pam Fanshaw, it's a
decision made from ambition not love. And
Rory has to wait ten years before Laura will
forgive him.

Now one of England's leading trainers, and
married to property tycoon Luke Mundy,
Laura asks Rory to ride her best horse,
Midnight Express, in Cheltenham's Two Mile
Champion Chase. Shortly afterwards, Luke is
killed on one of Laura's horses and she is
arrested for manslaughter. Rory won't desert
her this time and, setting out to prove Laura's
innocence, he discovers that there is more than
one person who will benefit from Luke's death.

Packed with intrigue and excitement, the plot
unravels at breakneck speed, revealing bribery,
blackmail and corruption as ingredients in this
highly accomplished racing thriller.

FICTION / CRIME 0 7472 4704 8

A selection of bestsellers from Headline

BODY OF A CRIME	Michael C. Eberhardt	£5.99	☐
TESTIMONY	Craig A. Lewis	£5.99	☐
LIFE PENALTY	Joy Fielding	£5.99	☐
SLAYGROUND	Philip Caveney	£5.99	☐
BURN OUT	Alan Scholefield	£4.99	☐
SPECIAL VICTIMS	Nick Gaitano	£4.99	☐
DESPERATE MEASURES	David Morrell	£5.99	☐
JUDGMENT HOUR	Stephen Smoke	£5.99	☐
DEEP PURSUIT	Geoffrey Norman	£4.99	☐
THE CHIMNEY SWEEPER	John Peyton Cooke	£4.99	☐
TRAP DOOR	Deanie Francis Mills	£5.99	☐
VANISHING ACT	Thomas Perry	£4.99	☐

All Headline books are available at your local bookshop or newsagent, or can be ordered direct from the publisher. Just tick the titles you want and fill in the form below. Prices and availability subject to change without notice.

Headline Book Publishing, Cash Sales Department, Bookpoint, 39 Milton Park, Abingdon, OXON, OX14 4TD, UK. If you have a credit card you may order by telephone – 01235 400400.

Please enclose a cheque or postal order made payable to Bookpoint Ltd to the value of the cover price and allow the following for postage and packing:

UK & BFPO: £1.00 for the first book, 50p for the second book and 30p for each additional book ordered up to a maximum charge of £3.00.

OVERSEAS & EIRE: £2.00 for the first book, £1.00 for the second book and 50p for each additional book.

Name ....

Address ....

....

....

If you would prefer to pay by credit card, please complete:
Please debit my Visa/Access/Diner's Card/American Express (delete as applicable) card no:

Signature .... Expiry Date ....